"What, no more icy w̶̶̶̶̶ ̶̶̶̶̶ with?"

Moses's gaze flicked to a nearby snow pile. "I suppose I'm not really safe, as there's still some form of frozen water around."

He wasn't surprised at Beth's quick recovery. She jerked her arms so fast across her chest that they bounced. "If you hope to get a warmer welcome, you'll need to look elsewhere. You won't find one from me."

"How do you know what I want to find with you?" Moses crossed his own arms.

She raised her chin. "Why are you here?"

Moses's jaw flexed. "Business." He wasn't going to admit that a good share of it was personal business. Personal business with her. She didn't seem... receptive to that topic at the moment.

"Why here? There're plenty of other states you could've expanded to. With all your businesses down south, surely you're needed there."

"Maybe I wanted to come home."

"This isn't your home anymore. It hasn't been for decades."

Moses smiled faintly. "Maybe I'd like it to be again."

Publishers Weekly bestselling author **Jocelyn McClay** grew up on an Iowa farm, ultimately pursuing a degree in agriculture. She met her husband while weight lifting in a small town—he "spotted" her. After thirty years in business management, they moved to an acreage in southeastern Missouri to be closer to family when their oldest of three daughters made them grandparents. When not writing, she keeps busy grandparenting, hiking, biking, gardening, quilting, knitting and substitute teaching.

Books by Jocelyn McClay

Love Inspired

The Amish Bachelor's Choice
Amish Reckoning
Her Forbidden Amish Love
Their Surprise Amish Marriage
Their Unpredictable Path
Her Unlikely Amish Protector
The Amish Spinster's Dilemma
Her Scandalous Amish Secret
Their Surprise Amish Reunion

Visit the Author Profile page at LoveInspired.com for more titles.

Their Surprise Amish Reunion

JOCELYN McCLAY

LOVE INSPIRED
INSPIRATIONAL ROMANCE

LOVE INSPIRED®
INSPIRATIONAL ROMANCE

ISBN-13: 978-1-335-59744-1

Their Surprise Amish Reunion

Copyright © 2024 by Jocelyn Ord

For questions and comments about the quality of this book, please contact us at CustomerService@Harlequin.com.

® is a trademark of Harlequin Enterprises ULC.

Love Inspired
22 Adelaide St. West, 41st Floor
Toronto, Ontario M5H 4E3, Canada
www.LoveInspired.com

Printed in Lithuania

MIX
Paper | Supporting responsible forestry
FSC® C021394

Trust in the Lord with all thine heart;
and lean not unto thine own understanding.
—*Proverbs* 3:5

Many thanks to Misti, Garrett, Ethan at 102 and the SF Health Department for sharing their knowledge. And Ursula, this book wouldn't have been possible without you.

Any mistakes are all on me.

Chapter One

"He ordered what?" Elizabeth Beiler scowled as she deftly seasoned the pot of green beans she was stirring. "Scrapple is not on the menu. It's never been on the menu." At least, not in the twenty-five or more years she'd worked at the Dew Drop restaurant. She hadn't made scrapple since... Her hand flexed around the lengthy spoon. Well, since a long, long time ago.

"He insisted." The young waitress, Rebecca, shrugged and spread her hands in a "what do you want me to do?" gesture.

"He what?" No one insisted in her restaurant. Well, it wasn't hers, actually. But in the months since the *Englisch* owners had moved out of state to be closer to their grown children's families, leaving the management of the Miller's Creek restaurant in her hands, it seemed like it was. Enough to dream it would soon be so. Enough that the savings she'd slowly, steadily been growing in those twenty-five-plus years, from when she'd started working here as a teenager, were now specifically earmarked "Dew Drop" instead of being just savings in general. The longer the restaurant remained unsold, the closer she figured—hoped—the gap between what she'd saved and what the owners would sell for would continue to diminish.

Elizabeth tapped the stainless steel counter, drawing

Rebecca's attention to where prepared plates waited under lights that kept pending orders warm. Wrinkling her nose at being caught not hustling as normal, the dark-haired waitress scooped up the plates with experienced hands and headed back through the swinging partial doors into the dining area.

Was it really going on two years that the restaurant had been for sale? Furrowing her brow, Elizabeth bent to open the oven door and check on the pans containing the daily special. A rush of heated air and the savory scent of roasted chicken and stuffing greeted her as she nodded in approval, gently closed the oven door and straightened, already moving to the next task. There was always another task.

Elizabeth had been frightened—*ach, nee,* not frightened. She didn't allow herself to be frightened. But she'd been considerably unsettled when the *Englisch* owners had informed her first, as their longest-serving employee—initially as a waitress and then as cook and baker with ever-increasing authority and responsibility—that they were planning to retire and were selling the restaurant.

Nodding stoically, she'd gone back to work, her hands steady as she'd diced and sliced, stirred, sifted and sautéed for the short remainder of the day. But driving home that evening, she'd felt her palms dampen the leather with sweat, and her fingers had been shaking on the reins. The restaurant for sale? Who would buy it? What would that do to her situation? Would the new owners give her the same authority and responsibility she'd worked for and earned over her years there? Easygoing and loose in their management style, the *Englisch* owners had been *gut* to work for. What if whoever bought the restaurant turned out to be overbearing? She'd have a hard time working in such an environment. She knew she was a little—*ach,* perhaps more than a little—

assertive. She didn't like to be controlled, and when folks tried to do so, it seemed everyone was unhappy with the results.

For a long time following the announcement of the sale, she'd gone to work every day braced for news of a buyer and the ensuing disruptions in her life.

But months had passed, now edging into years, with no sale. The scope of her job hadn't changed, but instead had increased to full management in addition to her other duties with the absentee owners. The prospect of the restaurant's sale, rather than causing a continuous knot in the pit of her stomach, was the source of excitement that grew with every additional dollar in her savings. The restaurant's availability was now the center of possibilities, opportunities, achievement, security—things Elizabeth had never before envisioned until the restaurant went up for sale.

She discounted the recent rumor that an out-of-town buyer had shown interest in the Dew Drop. Similar rumors had bubbled up before, only to fizzle out. In two months, maybe three, she'd have enough saved to broach the topic of buying it with the owners. Once they were in agreement, she'd approach Bishop Weaver about the subject. Surely he wouldn't object. He knew how well she ran the restaurant. It wasn't like she was a married woman and had a home and family to manage. Owning the restaurant, she'd have— outside of *Gott*, of course—control over her life.

"The special smells particularly *gut* today," Sadie, one of the other cooks in the collection of Amish and *Englisch* manning the kitchen, called from where she was prepping for the upcoming lunch rush. "I wouldn't have thought of making Amish Wedding Casserole."

Elizabeth inhaled deeply of the kitchen fragrances. It did smell *gut*. She knew the ovens worked more efficiently if she didn't open them, but doing so allowed aromas to escape and find their way into the restaurant's dining area. As to what had prompted her to plan the roasted chicken and celery-based stuffing dish as a special this week, she didn't know. It wasn't a usual choice, although ubiquitous at weddings—ergo its name. She'd helped prepare the dish in others' homes, frequently for a crowd. She'd supervised the preparations for it, along with homemade noodles, mashed potatoes and gravy, creamed celery and pepper slaw, when her twin sister had married last year.

Though as a spinster, it was a meal that'd never been prepared in her honor.

And why would that come to mind? Tucking a strand of dark brown hair that had dared escape back under her *kapp*, Elizabeth scowled. Maybe because of the scrapple. She'd made it, or *Pannhaas*, as it was sometimes called—a blend of pork scraps, trimmings, cornmeal and wheat flour that was molded, sliced and fried—for someone years ago. Someone she thought would be more…well, more than he'd ended up being.

Surely the requester wasn't… Hissing in a breath, Elizabeth jerked her hand from the hot surface she'd inadvertently rested it on. She darted a look at the door to the dining room before snorting softly. *Nee*, he'd never come back. If he'd cared enough, he'd have returned for her decades ago. Her stomach clenched at the memory of the days, months after his departure that she'd waited and hoped. Adamantly shaking her head, she adjusted the temperature under the pot of green beans. So what if he hadn't come back? She'd done fine without him.

Rebecca came through the swinging door, wearing a bemused smile that disappeared when Elizabeth's gaze sharpened on her.

"He's still requesting scrapple."

Elizabeth frowned. "Are they regulars?"

Miller's Creek was a small town. Most all of the Amish and *Englisch* who frequented the restaurant were known by name. Except for the daily special, several of the regular customers were so familiar with the Dew Drop they didn't even need a menu to order. It was doubtful they'd be requesting scrapple, which, while popular in Pennsylvania, wasn't so much here in Wisconsin. Besides, it was a time-consuming dish to make, and if they did have a hankering for it, they'd have put in an earlier request instead of ordering it out of the blue.

Rebecca shook her head. "*Nee*, I've never seen them before. It's two men in one of the booths, one older and one younger." Her dreamy smile reappeared. "And handsome."

Elizabeth rolled her eyes at Rebecca's words. The waitress, whom she'd worked with since the young woman had finished her Amish schooling a number of years ago, was like the daughter Elizabeth had never had. "We're interested in their appetites, not their looks."

Rebecca's smile expanded to a grin. "*Ja*, well, they look hungry. At least, the younger one does. They're Amish."

"I figured, with the scrapple request."

"Though I don't recognize the style of their hats."

Elizabeth grunted in understanding. To outsiders, all Amish hats, men's and women's, might look alike. But they weren't. Different Amish districts had different rules for apparel, including headgear. The *kapps* the women wore varied—material, length, stiffness, size or number of pleats, heart-shape versus straight-sided, etc. For men, hats from various districts differed in the height or shape of the crown—rounded or flat—and the assorted width of the brim. If Rebecca didn't recognize the hat style, the men weren't from any nearby Amish communities.

"Well, out-of-towners wouldn't know any better, I guess. Suggest something else and get on with their order." Elizabeth pulled one of the pans of daily special from an oven, grabbed a plate from a nearby pristine stack, scooped a steaming dollop onto it and handed it to Rebecca. "Have him try this. Tell him sorry, but no, on the scrapple and to quit asking about it."

She looked up in time to catch the young woman's smirk. "That's why you're out there and not me. You can be sweet. The only thing sweet about me is my baking." But there was a faint twinkle in her eye at the gruff comment. After watching Rebecca whisk back out the swinging door, Elizabeth shook her head as she turned in time to pull a pan of rolls out of another oven. No one would ever accuse her of being sweet. Having dealt with the rolls, she cast a quick glance around the smoothly running kitchen. Everything was well in hand for the upcoming rush.

Sweet? *Nee.* What she was was efficient. Industrious. Capable. Good things for a business owner, Elizabeth reminded herself as she adroitly plated an order. And why shouldn't she be one instead of just its manager? Her twin sister was a business owner. Granted, Emma's hat shop was a considerably smaller enterprise than the restaurant. But unlike what Emma now had, Elizabeth didn't have a husband and family at home to distract her. Since Emma's recent marriage, there was only Elizabeth at home. Emma had even taken the cat.

Elizabeth frowned as she gave the green beans another stir. Coming home to an empty house, where the glass of water she might've left on the counter in the morning was in its exact location when she walked in the door at the end of the day, was kind of lonely. Her frown deepened to a scowl. *If* one had time to be lonely.

It wasn't like she was truly alone. Emma still came a few days a week to work in her hat shop in the refurbished garage connected to the house the sisters used to share. But her hours were shorter and the days she worked fewer, so she could be home with her new husband and step-granddaughter. Elizabeth seldom saw her. Since Emma moved out, Elizabeth had increased her hours at the restaurant, spending even more time there. She liked it. She'd learned with Emma's romance and departure, albeit to just across the creek, that while she couldn't always control her personal life, she at least had control over her work one.

And she wasn't lonely. But maybe she'd give some thought to getting her own cat. Perhaps ask around to see if anyone had a kitten available. She hadn't paid much attention to her sister's cat, Willow, until the black-and-white tuxedoed feline had gone out the door with Emma. But now it would be nice to come home to…something in the house.

Rebecca burst through the swinging half doors.

"Did he like the chicken and stuffing?"

"*Ja*, but he asked what kind of restaurant refuses to take care of its customers. He still wants scrapple." Her eyes rounded and she took a step back, bumping into the doors and sending the hinges squeaking. "Um, if you're coming out to the dining room, you probably better leave the big spoon here."

"It's got a nice feel. Homey. Clean. Appropriate traffic flow. Decent crowd for this time of day. I'm still surprised you bought something sight unseen and I'm apprehensive about the distance from home. But as an operation, it could be a *gut* choice." The young man rested an arm along the back of the maroon vinyl booth as he scrutinized the restaurant's interior.

Moses Glick raised an eyebrow at his son's comment. "I'm surprised you noticed the surroundings. I was afraid all your attention was lost once your eyes latched on to the waitress."

"Well…" Daniel flashed a grin that, along with the younger man's brown hair and green eyes, Moses had been told was a replica of his own. Except, he grunted, for the gray that now streaked his own wavy locks. "She is a pretty one."

"You wouldn't want any of your sisters ogled like that when they waitress."

"My sisters don't look like that."

"Hmm. Maybe not to you."

Daniel winced and a flush crept up his cheeks as he glanced out the nearby window into the town's main street. "Seems like a nice community. Weather is cold, though. Things were blooming down in Ohio, but here they've still got a bit of snow on the ground."

Moses hid a smile at his son's abrupt change of subject. "It is. Or at least it was." He stroked a hand over the beard that indicated he was, or had been, a married man. "I have *wunderbar* memories of growing up here. Before my family moved to Ohio and…responsibilities took over."

"Why didn't you and *Mamm* ever come up to visit?"

"*Ach*, your *mamm* wasn't interested. I don't think she ever left Ohio in her lifetime." But here he was, a year after becoming a widower, returning to the area where he'd grown up. His lips twitched as Daniel's gaze again landed on the young waitress efficiently serving a nearby table. Tipping his head, Moses studied the girl himself. Her deft movements and quick smile reminded him of someone else he'd seen waitress years ago in this restaurant. Except for the quick smile. His girl hadn't been a smiler. More a scowler.

He'd always loved to tease her and make that scowl appear. Then he'd work on coaxing a smile out. As they'd been rare, and sincere, they'd been very precious.

Was that why he'd come all this way? Because of a woman he couldn't forget? Moses scowled at himself. He'd come because of a business opportunity too good to pass up. If it happened to be in a community in which he had fond memories, well, that was even better. He'd worked many years taking care of others. Was it wrong to take this chance for himself?

He pressed a hand against a stomach that churned with tension rather than hunger. It might be, if the financial risk he'd taken to do so affected his other operations. Because failure wasn't an option. He'd never failed before, even when times were difficult. Too many were depending on him to continue to succeed.

The waitress returned, still smiling but more apprehensively as she whisked a plate from in front of him.

"What's with the scrapple?" Daniel, reluctantly tearing his gaze from the departing waitress, frowned. "I've never seen you order it before. We don't serve it in our restaurants." His eyebrows rose until they disappeared under his bangs. "And that was pretty rude. I hope our customers never treat us like that."

"I haven't had scrapple in a long time. I've kind of had a...hankering for it lately."

Moses straightened at the bang from the back of the restaurant. He grinned, the creases in his cheeks matching the fine lines at the corners of his eyes, as a woman, sturdy and on the short side, came sailing from the kitchen area. He pivoted in his seat, resting one elbow on the smooth wooden table and the other on the booth's back, as he watched her approach. When she saw him, her pace halted so abruptly the young waitress trailing in her wake dodged to keep from running into her. His grin expanded as the older woman's chin lowered, her still-smooth skin stretched over an obviously gritted jaw, and she surged forward again to stand, fists on hips, in front of their booth. Her brown-eyed gaze locked with his.

"Hello, Beth. So you don't make scrapple anymore?"

His heartbeat, surprisingly loud—and galloping like a runaway horse—ticked off the moments as she stared at him. As she stepped closer to the table, Moses drew in a breath. He held it, mesmerized, as a hint of a smile touched her lips. Focused on that promising expression, he neglected the hand that reached for his glass of ice water. His eyes widened as the water, cold as the reluctantly departing winter, splashed into his lap.

Chapter Two

M oses lurched out of the booth, shedding ice cubes that fell *tink, tink, tink* to slide across the wooden floor. Rebecca's and Daniel's eyes and mouths gaped like fish that had just been jerked from a pond. Tugging the legs of his broadfall pants, which felt like they'd been dipped in a Wisconsin river in January, away from him, Moses heard more ice hit the floor as Elizabeth pivoted without a word.

He watched her straight back as she marched to the kitchen, a smile tilting the corner of his mouth. Whatever else he might find up here, at least Beth hadn't changed.

"Oh! Oh, I'm so sorry!" If the waitress's eyes grew any wider, they'd vie for size with the plate-covering pancakes that he'd seen go by. "It was an…" She struggled a moment for an appropriate explanation of what it was. "Accident?" she finished weakly.

Moses didn't argue. He was well aware accidental spills frequently occurred in restaurants. This hadn't been one of them.

Grabbing a wad of napkins from a nearby dispenser, the waitress thrust them in his direction. She snatched another handful and quickly began mopping up the booth seat and surrounding floor, aided by Daniel, who'd leaped up to assist. Dabbing at his pants, Moses raised a dubious eyebrow at his son, wondering if Daniel's enthusiastic involvement was more related to impressing the young woman rather than helping his father.

The dark-haired waitress retrieved a small tub to contain the sopping napkins. While simultaneously loading the tub, Daniel's hand brushed hers. They froze as their eyes met. Moses shook his head as he slid back into the now dry booth. *Oh, to be young again.* He snagged his coat from the corner of the booth, where it'd thankfully escaped the flood, and draped it over his lap.

He narrowed his gaze at the back of the restaurant, where Beth had disappeared. Was she married now? It was hard to tell, as Amish didn't wear wedding rings. Married Amish women traditionally seldom worked outside the home, as caring for family and household was a worthy and necessary occupation in itself. But more and more married Amish women were now working in and owning businesses—quilt shops, craft stores, soap and lotion shops and produce markets among them—that her employment here wasn't necessarily a sign she was single. And Beth—at least, the Beth he used to know—probably would've had the same reaction in response to his teasing whether she was married or not.

While discussing the restaurant's sale, he'd asked the owners about existing employees. They'd promoted the restaurant as a good place to work, as they'd had some employees for years. Elizabeth, but not her last name, had been mentioned. The prospect that she still worked here had been a tipping point in buying a restaurant in his hometown. On paper, it was a *gut* investment. Too *gut* to pass up. Particularly when he'd been looking for a reason to return? By appearances thus far, it still seemed so. But still, the action had been a risky venture for such a foolish notion as homesickness for a place…or a person.

The commotion at their booth had drawn the interest of other diners. From every corner of the dining area, necks were craned in his direction. A few brows, ones already wrinkled with the passage of time, creased further as they gazed at him before lifting in recognition and nodding. Moses nodded back. Some he recognized. With others, names to go with the faces flitted just out of reach. It'd been decades since he was last here.

One man pushed up from the table where he'd been sitting and strode over. Moses furrowed his own brow, striving to recognize the features above the chest-length, graying beard. His expression clearing, he smiled at the approaching man. Though Ezekiel Weaver had been older than he, he'd been on good terms with the bishop before Moses's family had left the community.

At least, he hoped so. Surreptitiously Moses tugged at his coat, ensuring it covered his lap.

Daniel and the waitress launched back into cleaning up the spill when the bishop stopped at the side of the booth.

"So the restaurant sale is final?"

Moses's glass, fortunately empty, clattered back onto the tabletop when it slipped from the waitress's fingers. Her face flushing, she hastily snatched it up to drop it into the tub of soggy napkins.

"*Ja.* Confirmed just the other day."

Ezekiel stroked a hand through his beard. "Before we talked, the *Englisch* owners had also left me a message to call them. They wanted to make sure it was all right for a restaurant in our district to be Amish-owned."

Moses understood. Though many restaurants served "Amish" food and employed Amish personnel, due to the needed technology, government regulations and long hours away from family required to run one, few restaurants were actually owned by Old Order Amish. If they did have a restaurant, it was more of a serve-in-the-home operation. As the growing Amish population was expanding beyond its agricultural base, business ownership of that nature was becoming slightly less taboo, but it depended on the district's leadership. To own an establishment like this one, approval of the community's bishop and ministers was a necessary step. He needed to stay on this man's good side.

"We started out with a bakery in Ohio. With church leadership approval and *Gott*'s blessing, it grew from there."

The bishop looked around the dining room. Many of the tables were filling as lunchtime approached. "It's a *gut* business here. An important one in our community. The *Englisch* owners worked to accommodate our way of life as much as possible." Ezekiel turned his attention back to Moses. "We expect it will remain that way."

Moses held the older man's hooded gaze. "Absolutely."

Nodding, the bishop stepped back to let the waitress whisk the tub off the table and, with a wary look over her shoulder, head toward the kitchen. "Welcome back." Ezekiel tilted his head toward where he'd been sitting. "I'll return to my meal and let you get back to yours. I'll talk with you later."

Moses didn't have a meal yet to return to. After his ice bath, he wasn't sure he'd get one. Particularly after the waitress reached the kitchen and shared her news with the head cook. His smile at the thought of Beth's face when she heard it crumpled as his eyes widened. Stifling a wince, he fisted his hand to keep from raising it to his chest where pain, something he'd recently become acutely familiar with, generated. *Not now. Don't let this be the one.* Closing his eyes, Moses concentrated on his breathing. *Take a breath. Hold it. Let it out. Take a breath...*

"Are you all right?"

Moses opened his eyes to his son's frowning regard. He swallowed, willing the pain to fade away. "*Ja.* Just trying not to shiver after my ice bath."

Daniel's skeptical gaze remained on him for a moment before his son's face relaxed into a smile. "Looks like she really didn't want to make scrapple."

Moses forced his lips to lift in return. "Doesn't appear so." Relieved he could finally draw a full breath, Moses retrieved a few more napkins from the dispenser and pressed them against the damp leg of his triblend denim pants.

Daniel glanced toward where Beth and the waitress had disappeared. "She might be a *gut* cook. But her demeanor with customers needs a little work."

Moses ran a hand over the back of his neck. He'd known Beth would respond to provocation. And he'd provoked her anyway, just like he always had. But today, his unexpected presence alone would've been provoking enough. "It's not all her fault." He cleared his throat. "Beth and I… we have a history."

Jaw sagging, his son stared at him as if he'd just sprouted another head. Moses scowled. Did Daniel think he'd had no life prior to becoming his father? Sliding out of the booth, Moses stood, positioning the coat to block evidence of the spill. If she'd greeted him with a dousing of cold water, what would Beth do when she discovered he was now her boss? Or was that what'd prompted the deluge? Had the owners told her of the restaurant's sale? Either way, it was time he and Beth had a conversation.

Ja, they had a history. But he'd come back to find out whether they could finally have a future. Squaring his shoulders, Moses headed for the kitchen.

* * *

Though she longed to send them rocking on their hinges to match her rioting senses, Elizabeth instead slipped with iron control through the kitchen doors.

He was back. Moses was back. She took two strides into the soothing confines of her domain and stopped. Why? Had he finally come back for her? Inhaling the comfortable scents of the kitchen, she was perturbed to discover she was shaking. She hadn't seen him for years. Decades.

Not since the day she'd told him she wouldn't marry him.

Her heartbeat ran rampant as she stared unseeing at the normal bustle that surrounded her. Well, if he was back, he was too late. Too late for him, and, from the beard that shaded his neck, marking him as a married man, too late for her. Due to Rebecca's glowing description, Elizabeth had spared Moses's companion a brief glance, only to barely refrain from gaping at the young man's resemblance to the one who'd courted her decades earlier. Moses had obviously long ago married someone else. Married and had a family. A family that could've been hers. After her halting refusal, he'd never even tried to change her mind. Had he mourned her loss at all? Or had he simply wed the first girl he'd met after moving to Ohio? Elizabeth widened her eyes, which for some reason burned at the backs.

No wonder he'd never returned. Why should he, when he'd dropped her like a dirty dish towel?

She should've known. It was no more than she'd expected. Much as he'd insinuated otherwise, Moses hadn't cared for her as much as she'd…thought of him. Still, it…hurt. Marching to the counter, she pulled a knife from its companions along the pristine, magnetized metal strip. Surely there were potatoes or something to peel. There was always something to peel, chop, slice or dice. Leaning against the stainless steel sink, she kept her back to the bustling room.

Nee, it didn't hurt. Hurting would mean he'd had enough control over her to affect her feelings. She'd been…a little disappointed. That was all. He'd said he'd loved her. She pressed her lips together to cease their trembling. That must've been a farce, as quickly as he'd moved on. Her glance dropped to the keen-edged blade. It, along with her hand, was shaking. With a sigh, she stuck it back on the strip with a *snick*. Working with a knife just now wasn't a good idea. Not if she needed to keep all her fingers in working order.

Still, work was her refuge. She snatched up nearby pot holders, opened the oven door and grabbed the edge of the pan of golden-brown rolls, only to drop it with a clatter when she misjudged her grip on the pot holders and touched hot metal. Elizabeth stared in dismay at the collection of rolls that had tumbled to the floor.

The kitchen commotion faded as the rest of the staff cast her wary glances. Scowling, Elizabeth rearranged the pot holders and transferred the remaining pan of rolls from oven to counter before kneeling to collect the tumbled rolls from the floor and drop them into the trash.

She was at the sink running cold water over her hand when Rebecca, clutching a tub of soaked napkins, burst into the kitchen.

"He bought the restaurant."

Elizabeth turned off the faucet, certain that, with the running water, she'd misheard the breathless words. Grabbing a paper towel, she turned to face the wide-eyed woman. "What?"

"That man, the one you dumped the water on, he bought the restaurant."

Elizabeth's brisk hand-drying slowed to a halt. Her brows lowered. "But I… That's not possi—" The damp paper towel crumpled in her fist. "Why do you say that? How do you know?"

"He and Bishop Weaver were talking about it."

"The restaurant has been for sale for so long, surely they were just talking about the possibility." Elizabeth didn't know how she got the words through her numb lips. Lead was congregating in her stomach. Cold, cold lead that sent a chill expanding up to her chest and extending into her limbs.

"Nee." The waitress shook her head so hard her white prayer *kapp* slipped off-center. "They said it was already final."

Lightheaded, Elizabeth crossed her arms over her chest and slumped against the sink. "No. No, you must've misunderstood."

All activity in the kitchen stopped. The only sound was the sizzle of a few hamburgers on the grill. Elizabeth knew everyone was, like her, staring at Rebecca. The young woman shook her head again, more slowly this time. "I…don't… think so," she said, even though her face revealed she wished she was wrong.

Suddenly hot and sweaty, with bile scalding the back of her throat, Elizabeth whirled to face the sink. With her knees threatening to fold, she braced her hands on the edge. How could the owners, whom she'd worked for all these years, do this to her? Surely they knew she wanted to buy it? Her fingers tightened until the tips were white against the sink's smooth lip. Surely they—

But they didn't know. She hadn't told them, keeping her ambition secret, wanting to wait until—certain her offer would be accepted—she had all the money in place.

Hunching over the sink, she stared into its pristine depth,

the stainless steel so shiny she could almost see her outline in it. She forced a swallow against the menacing nausea. She couldn't be sick. If she was, she'd just have to clean and scour the sink. No time for that with a busy hour bearing down on them. If she was sick, those in the kitchen might suspect she had a weakness. Stiffening her elbows, she pushed upright.

Abandoning the sink, Elizabeth found her staff standing as if they'd been flash frozen in a Wisconsin winter, complete with white faces. With a slow inhalation, she surveyed her coworkers, many of whom she'd worked with for years. "We've got customers. Unless we want them to come in here and serve themselves, we need to get to it." At her words, and the look she touched on each of them, the kitchen burst back into action.

Despite her bravado, her stomach churned like the nearby industrial mixer and her mind darted like a bee trapped in a jar. She started toward a stainless steel counter, but the buzzing bee made it impossible to think of the next step in any process. Unclenching her hands, Elizabeth glanced in surprise at the paper towel still wadded in one.

She drifted toward the large trash bin, her stride becoming purposeful when she saw it was nearly full. Here was something she could do. Suddenly, the normally soothing sanctuary of her—she grimaced—*the* kitchen was intolerable. She needed to get away. Even if only for a brief moment. Reaching the trash bin, she jerked the inside liner away from its edges and yanked the bag out of the large plastic container. Automatically twisting the loose ends of the plastic to tie a quick knot, she carried the bag to the rear of the restaurant. As she swept out the back door, she knew there was only one person to blame for this unexpected turmoil in her life.

I should've dumped a whole pitcher of ice water on him instead of just a glass. Rerouted the Fox and Wisconsin Rivers to wash him back to where he came from.

It was all Moses Glick's fault. Years ago, he'd destroyed one dream by leaving. Now he'd wrecked another upon his return. Elizabeth thinned her lips. This time when he left, which couldn't be soon enough to suit her, she'd greet his departure with cheers instead of tears.

The heavy door banged behind her, closing off the heat of the kitchen. She sucked in a lungful of crisp early spring air. If turmoil hadn't been keeping her warm, it would've been downright chilly. Despite the cold, Elizabeth welcomed the sudden, seeming peacefulness. A tear trickled down her cheek. Hissing in a breath, she rapidly blinked her eyes. It was the change from warm kitchen to abrupt cold that was causing the leak, not anything as weak as hurt or disappointment. Dashing the moisture away with her free hand, she started across the alley, only to stumble as she barely avoided stepping into a large pothole, one that'd been growing over the long Wisconsin winter.

Gritting her teeth, Elizabeth kicked a broken chunk of pavement into the crater on her way past. She'd mentioned the pothole to the absentee owners a few times earlier this winter. They'd assured her they'd address it with the township, but it still wasn't fixed. It needed to be soon, before it caused more than just an eyesore and inconvenience. Rebecca had misjudged the hole upon leaving once last week and had driven over it. The resultant jarring had brought her scrambling down from the buggy to ensure she hadn't damaged one of her wooden wheels.

Elizabeth cast a quick, longing glance at her own buggy. At the allure of harnessing her mare and heading home, she drifted a few steps in that direction before she pivoted. Avoiding problems never solved anything. Trash bag bumping against her leg, she marched to the walled-in structure across the alley, unlatched the gate and swung it wide enough to slip through with her load. The dumpster's metal lid creaked when she lifted it to drop the bag with a thud into its empty depths. Letting the lid fall back down with a bang, Elizabeth brushed her hands off, wishing she could wipe Moses Glick out of her life again as easily. Instead of heading for the gate, she stopped behind it, out of sight of anyone in the alley, then drooped against the enclosure's wooden fence and closed her eyes. Avoiding problems might not solve anything. But she'd never been as tempted to do so as she was today.

Moses stepped through the swinging door into the restaurant's kitchen, an environment as familiar to him as the front porch of his house. He automatically took in the efficient layout and shiny clean equipment of the area. His experienced nose identified grilled beef, roasted chicken, the yeasty smell of fresh rolls and the faint residual of some kind of sweet baked items. The myriad of smells remained, but the cacophony of noise ceased at his entrance when all work stopped. Searching the faces turned in his direction, he didn't see the one he was looking for.

By the collective stares, he was the obvious interloper. Tempted to shift his feet and hunch his shoulders, he instead smiled and nodded. These were now his employees. *Begin as you mean to go on.* His efforts were rewarded with a few tentative ones in return. But only a few.

Sighing inwardly, Moses held his smile. "Where is she?"

There was no question as to who *she* was. In unison, heads either tipped or looked in the direction of the back door. Nodding in satisfaction, Moses wove his way through the area to the rear entrance. If he knew Beth, she wouldn't have gone far. She wasn't the type to back down from a confrontation. After passing through the reinforced door into the alley, he gently closed it behind him. Straight ahead was a small, walled-in enclosure, the partially open gate revealing a glimpse of a large green dumpster. A woman stepped from inside the enclosure to pull the gate closed and hook the latch.

Apparently, the rattle of the gate and click of the latch obscured his footfalls, because when she turned around and saw him, Beth jumped near a foot and pressed her hands to her chest.

His gaze locked with her brown eyes. "What, no more icy water to douse me with?" Moses's gaze flicked to a nearby snow pile. "I suppose I'm not really safe, as there's still some form of frozen water around."

He wasn't surprised at Beth's quick recovery. She jerked her arms so fast across her chest that they bounced. "If you hope to get a warmer welcome, you'll need to look elsewhere. You won't find one from me."

"How do you know what I want to find with you?" Moses crossed his own arms, the action lifting the coat in his hand away from pants where the fabric, though now only slightly damp, was still wet enough to quickly chill.

She raised her chin. "Why are you here?"

His jaw flexed. "Business." He wasn't going to admit that a good share of it was personal business. Personal business with her. She didn't seem…receptive to that topic at the moment.

Her chin crept higher. "And about that. You bought my restaurant." In the crisp air, her voice echoed down the alley.

This matter, at least, he could talk about. "Yours, Beth? I bought it from some *Englischers*. And I'm in the restaurant business."

"Go be in the restaurant business back wherever you came from. Don't you have enough there to keep you busy?"

If her chin rose any higher, she'd be staring at the puffy clouds drifting by overhead. "Ah, Beth. It's Ohio, as you well know. I doubt that you forget anything you don't want to forget. And *ja*, I have two restaurants there, but being a businessman, I look for opportunities to expand my operations."

"Why here? There're plenty of other states you could've expanded to instead of Wisconsin. And my restaurant."

"This was the one that was for sale." Apparently, the owners hadn't advised Beth that the Dew Drop had been sold. The omission was unfortunate, but she had to have known it would happen at some point. For sure and certain, his appearance was a shock. Still, she knew him. Unlike having some stranger buy it, at least Beth knew he could be trusted. She should be glad.

"I was going to buy it."

Moses's brows shot up at her declaration. "Were you now. Did you have the money?"

She scowled. "Almost."

"How about the bishop's approval? He didn't seem enthusiastic having it Amish-owned. And I imagine even less so owned by an Amish woman."

Her scowl deepened. Moses took that to mean the answer was no. He wasn't surprised. Bishop Weaver's attitude made him think he'd have to tiptoe around the man himself. If *he* needed to tiptoe regarding the business, an Amish woman probably wouldn't even be able to get a foot in the door.

"I can understand why you'd be interested. It looks like a *gut* investment, *if* it's been managed effectively."

Beth puffed up like an agitated chicken at his words. "It's been managed quite fine, thank you." Her eyes drilled him.

"Now you can be an absentee owner like the *Englisch* ones were. With all your businesses down south, surely you're needed there."

"Maybe I wanted to come home."

"This isn't your home anymore. It hasn't been for decades."

Moses smiled faintly. "Maybe I'd like it to be again."

Beth's gaze remained locked with his as, keeping her distance, she skirted around him toward the restaurant's back door. "Well, you aren't needed here. The Dew Drop is a well-run establishment. There's not a single thing that needs changed, because I—" The last ended on a yelp as she crumpled to the ground.

Moses darted forward to where she sprawled, grabbing her ankle, at the side of a large pothole.

Crouching beside her, he reached for her, only to halt under her glare.

"Now look what you made me do!"

"Me! I was standing five feet away, hoping my damp pants wouldn't freeze solid while you stomped off."

Beth was obviously struggling to simultaneously hold her glower against the pain and stand without his help. A grimace leaked through. She began to collapse, this time not complaining as Moses folded his arms about her, supporting her as she sagged back to the ground.

"Your ankle?" He reached out to run a hand over the thick black hose she wore to check for injuries before thinking better of it.

"*Ja*. You made me sprain it." The grumpy words had lost their previous intensity. She was hurting indeed. But though she started to shiver, Beth shrugged off his arms.

Frowning, Moses scooted back. With a sigh, he draped his coat around her, relieved she didn't shake that off as well. Squatting at her level, he waited until she met his gaze. "Beth."

"Don't call me that." But it was said without heat. She closed her eyes, chagrin evident on her face. "Oh, all right. I should've watched where I was going. It's not like I didn't know the pothole was there."

He grinned at what for her was a major capitulation. "Are you going to let me help you?"

Her ankle throbbed. Elizabeth barely stifled a whimper. She wanted so badly to lean against Moses. To again feel his strong, capable arms about her. The immediately remembered scents that rose from the coat now keeping her warm were bad enough. But she'd depended on him once. It'd been a mistake. It wouldn't happen again.

Her eyes daring him to help her, she pushed awkwardly to her feet. Balancing on her good leg, she brushed grit from her hands. "I don't need your help. I can take care of myself."

The words were barely out of her mouth when the restaurant's back door creaked open and Rebecca poked her head out. When the waitress spied Elizabeth, her expression lightened and she blew out a long breath.

"Anna's younger brother called from the phone shack. The reason Anna is late is because she's sick and can't come in to waitress. And it's…um…it's getting pretty busy in here. If you want to come back in and…and help?" Her gaze shifted uncertainly between the two of them. With a tentative smile, she ducked back inside, the resultant bang of the door echoing down the cold alley.

Elizabeth's quick step toward the door almost had her crumpling to the ground again. They were a waitress short going into lunchtime. Someone could be redeployed from the kitchen, but that would leave them shorthanded there.

She bit her lip. Already the skin was tightening around her ankle as it swelled. Much as she wanted to deny it, with restricted movements, she wouldn't be a lot of help. Sitting on a stool in one location, she could do some tasks, but not enough to support what needed to be done in the next while. And then there was the evening meal. Her unscheduled workers didn't carry cell phones and it could be some time before they got a message from the phone shack.

If the restaurant's service and reputation over the next while were going to meet her standards, she was going to need some assistance. Her gaze reluctantly cut to where Moses stood, arms crossed over his broad chest. She met his raised eyebrow with a scowl.

"You reconsidering that offer of help, Beth?"

Chapter Three

Elizabeth drew in a slow breath. "I suppose an extra set of hands wouldn't go amiss at the moment. If you know what you're doing," she added darkly.

"I'll try not to oversalt the potatoes or underfry the hamburgers." Though Moses smiled, it was a sympathetic one as, eyeing her ankle, he hastened to the door and pushed it wide.

Gritting her teeth, Elizabeth headed toward it with a heavy limp. In addition to the aroma of the roasted chicken casserole competing with that of fresh rolls, the subdued clatter of cookware and muted voices met her at the doorway. Heads lifted and jaws dropped as she hobbled into the kitchen. Gazes darted from her to Moses, who'd followed her inside.

"What happened to you?" The metal spoon clanked against the plate as Sadie simultaneously added a serving of casserole and a roll.

"Whoa…" The *Englisch* teenager running the dishwasher accidentally sprayed water onto the floor.

"It's nothing." Elizabeth swept her hand in front of her. "I just rolled my ankle in the pothole out there. One that should've been fixed sometime back. If someone will grab me one of the stools from the back of the pantry just in case I need to occasionally sit for a bit, I can fill plates."

Rebecca came through the swinging door with a tray of

dishes. Setting them in the staging area for the dishwasher, she turned to the line for the next available order. Pausing, she glanced from face to face of her immobile coworkers before her eyes cut to where Elizabeth was lurching behind the stainless steel counter, using its edge for support.

"Rebecca, right?"

The waitress jerked her round-eyed attention from Elizabeth to Moses. "Tell my son I need him back here." The directive was tempered with a smile. Rebecca's expression eased and, grinning in return, she collected the next order and swept back out the door.

"No stool. You need somewhere to get that foot elevated."

Elizabeth opened her mouth to tell him her opinion regarding his unwanted decree but, observing the intrigued expressions around her, closed it with a snap. "I can't do that." She gestured to the congested confines of the kitchen. "What am I going to do? Prop my foot up on the prep table? Or maybe the stove?"

Moses responded to her sarcasm with what seemed to be his habitual expression, another smile, one that brought her no pleasure. Particularly when he added, "I didn't say it would be in here."

For a moment, the growing ache in her ankle was masked by the flush of heat and alarm that swept through her. He hadn't taken ten steps in her kitchen and already he was taking charge, overruling her decisions. Though she clenched her teeth at the effort, Elizabeth shifted her weight between both feet and stood up to her full height, minimal against his though it was.

"The ink of your signature can hardly be dry and you're already bossing everyone around."

She inhaled sharply through her nostrils when he responded with another smile. "*Nee.* I'm trying to ensure that you get back on your feet as soon as you can. Which means keeping the swelling down as much as possible. So—" Moses glanced into a room off the kitchen—little more than a broom closet—just big enough for a desk, chair, file cabinet and bulletin boards, which was used for an office. "If you'll sit in here with your foot up on the desk, that should keep your ankle above your heart."

He was already trying to get her out of the way. "But I can't help in there. I can't see all that's going on."

"Don't your people know what to do?"

"Of course they do." Her posture was as stiff as her ankle was getting.

"Then why do you need to see? You can hear everything. And if there're any questions, you're still right here in the middle of the action." Moses looked over when Daniel, his brow creased and his eyes curious, slipped through the swinging door. "Now sit down so everyone can get back to work and take care of our customers."

Elizabeth huffed. When everyone stared at her without contradicting him, she pivoted on her good leg and used the doorjamb to support her way into the cubbyhole before plunking down into the worn office chair.

At least he didn't say "my" customers. Elizabeth glowered at the neatly organized items that fringed the battered desk. Being off her feet did feel better, not that she'd admit it. And despite her claim, when she inched her chair slightly to the side, she still had sight, though limited, into the kitchen. Having tucked the edges of her skirt under her, Elizabeth gripped her knee with both hands and tentatively lifted it to rest the foot of her throbbing ankle on the desktop, careful not to wrinkle the large calendar, its daily blocks jotted with neatly written notes, that took up a good share of it.

She stifled an escaping sigh of relief when Moses appeared in the doorway, a bag of ice in one hand and a small stack of white towels in the other.

He lifted the bag. "Rice."

She gave him a withering look. "I don't know how you're making it in the restaurant business. That's ice, not rice."

With a grin, Moses squeezed into the room. "Rest, ice, compression and elevate. RICE. Courtesy of years of first aid training with the local fire department. I didn't see any compression bandages in the first aid kit." Elizabeth pressed her lips together under his pointed gaze. "It's something we'll need to get added. You never know when they might come in handy." Using one of the towels to wrap the ice bag, he put it with the other towels on the desktop. After a brief hesitation, he gently lifted her ankle to set it on the newly made cushion.

At Elizabeth's sharp inhalation, a grimace crossed his face. "I'm sorry. I know it has to hurt." With continued care, he arranged the draped ice bag over her ankle. "Direct from in here. But keep that foot elevated." With a rueful smile, he eased past her to the door.

Seconds after he disappeared from the doorway, Elizabeth heard him ask where he needed to jump in. She drew in a careful breath, glad for a moment to be out of sight of curious glances. Glad Moses had taken her response as a reaction to the pain and not the gentle touch of his hands. Although she shivered at the cold already seeping through the ice pack, she grudgingly acknowledged her heel felt better cushioned instead of propped directly on the desk's hard surface.

But effectively attending to an ankle wasn't the same as efficiently running a restaurant.

Still, she raised an eyebrow at Moses's instruction to his son to bus tables since he didn't know the menu, so that Rebecca had more time for orders. She raised the other when he told Daniel to review the table diagram so he could start delivering prepared orders. Surely no one could memorize the chart so fast, but from what she could see of the younger Glick's comings and goings beyond the office door, he seemed to be doing well enough. At least complaints from disgruntled customers over wrong order deliveries weren't reported back to the kitchen. And she was listening for them.

In fact, they all seemed to be doing well enough. *Without her.* Despite her expectation, there were few, if any, harried calls to her from the kitchen. Moses was expediting orders, doing whatever needed to be done. Working with *her* team. Who were responding as if his presence, and not hers, was an everyday occurrence.

The old chair creaked as Elizabeth slumped against its back. So much for her worry about her staff. For her instinctive inclination to challenge Moses should he even think about letting one of them go. From the sounds of the busy but cheerful communication beyond the office door, they were ready to make him Employer of the Year.

Elizabeth's fingers, curled around the worn brown leather that padded the chair's arms, tightened until the knuckles were white. Would she be the first, and only, to go, then? They were making it through a shorthanded rush hour without her.

Moses had proved he didn't care much—or enough—for her years ago. She'd been hollowed out when he'd left her. He'd say it had been her choice. But what choice had there been between a beau whose devotion she'd doubted and a family who needed her? So she'd given him a test, foolishly thinking he'd return for her. She'd almost considered following him. She, who never reexamined her decisions, had wondered if she'd made the wrong decision in staying. But time had gone on, and on, and years had passed.

He'd failed the test. Obviously, she'd made the right decision.

But it'd been a painful one. How had she let him have so much control over her? In public, she hadn't batted an eye at his departure. In private, she'd wept copious tears. Useless tears. Elizabeth had vowed after those woeful hours that no one would have that kind of control over her again.

Particularly Moses Glick.

And here he was, taking over her kitchen while he stuck her in a closet.

The noise beyond the doorway was fever pitch in what Elizabeth knew was the climax of the busy lunch hour. Leaning forward in the chair, she swept the ice bag from her ankle. She lowered her foot to the floor, wincing as her heel connected with a thud that sent pain reverberating through her ankle. She hobbled to the door, only to be directed back inside by a chorus of voices. Hunching her shoulders, she stiffly returned to her assigned cubbyhole, fretting her lower lip at her diminished stature. With an irritated grunt, she resettled her foot, snagged a notebook off the desk and began working on next week's specials and planning her orders, though with an ear to the kitchen, it was taking twice as long as it normally did. Gradually, the frantic pace beyond the little room slowed.

"How are you doing?"

Elizabeth dropped the notebook into her lap with a start when Moses filled the doorway. He should've looked silly, with a net over his now hatless dark hair and another one entrapping his beard, a beard trimmed shorter than that of a man married twenty-some years should be. Apparently, it wasn't only the winters that were shorter in Ohio. The beards were allowed to be as well. For sure and certain, Bishop Weaver wouldn't approve of a beard of any length tucked inside a net. For sure and certain, she shouldn't either, but the subdued hair on his head and jawline only made his smiling green eyes all the more striking.

A white apron, the brightness of the material in sharp contrast to the strong neck that was still tanned dark from apparent hours in the sun—how did he get time in the sun when running a restaurant?—looped around his neck and covered his shirt and pants to midthigh.

"Do you need anything?"

Elizabeth folded her arms over her chest and scowled at her black-stockinged foot propped on top of her desk, sticking out like a…a turkey leg on a tray of delicate cookies. She braced herself to drop it to the floor, lifting her ankle an inch off the white towels before pausing. Since when had she worried about her appearance?

And do I need anything? I need to have you out of my restaurant. And back out of my life. "I need to get out there and be productive." As she caught the whine in her voice, heat climbed up her cheeks.

"Other than that." Her grumble rolled right off Moses's netted hair and down to where she presumed his apron was tied. Rubbing a hand over his mouth, he eyed her ankle. "How is it feeling? Do you want someone to take you home?"

Was he trying to completely get her out of the picture, now that it was *his* restaurant? "*Nee.* We're shorthanded enough as it is. I don't want to take anyone away from their work when we need to be preparing for tonight's crowd. But the ice bag is leaking."

"I'll get you a fresh one." He grinned as he lifted the dripping bag from her ankle. "At least the ice I applied to you is contained and not splashed all over your lap."

Elizabeth's lips twitched in response before she tightened them. Moses returned shortly with a fresh bag, deftly replacing damp towels with dry ones and gently rearranging her ankle upon them.

"Gut?"

"Tolerable." Elizabeth didn't lift her eyes from the employee schedule she stared at without seeing a single name. Moses gave an amused snort and slipped back out the door.

An hour later, Elizabeth hobbled out to check on the prep work for the evening meal. Although her staff smiled at her and asked how she was doing, no one suggested she remain in the kitchen. She limped back to the office, elevating her foot though not her spirits as she listened to the growing comradery in the kitchen between her staff and the new owner. Although focused on Moses's voice, Elizabeth furrowed her brow at the conversations between Rebecca and Daniel. If she didn't know it was a restaurant kitchen beyond the doorway, with the dove-like cooing going on between the two young folks, she'd almost think she was in a barn.

Elizabeth drummed her fingers on the arm of the chair. She needed to warn Rebecca. The girl had sense—surely she knew enough not to fall for a handsome face just because he paid attention to her?

She scowled. So what was her excuse for doing the same thing decades ago?

Like his father, who would surely soon return to his wife and restaurants down south, it was doubtful the son was staying. To get attached would only bring Rebecca grief when the boy returned to Ohio. Elizabeth knew the girl, knew how close she was to her *mamm* and family. Rebecca wouldn't leave. And when he did, she'd spend the next long years wondering...

The least Elizabeth could do was protect her. Keep her from making a mistake. If need be, she'd somehow get the Glick men to leave before she...before Rebecca was hurt.

After what seemed like a fortnight instead of an afternoon, she heard it mentioned just after seven that the last customer had left and the front door was locked. The sounds in the kitchen drifted off as her staff tidied up and put the restaurant to bed until Monday, the next business day. The *Englisch* owners had either understood working on the Lord's Day was frowned upon or couldn't get the labor to do so. One by one, her employees poked their head in the office door for a moment to say good-night and commiserate on how she was doing.

Bed was where Elizabeth longed to be as well. Sitting against her bird's-eye maple headboard with a pillow propped under her ankle, which was aching with the ferocity of a continuously boiling pot. Her lips twisted. How could she be so exhausted when all she'd done was sit? Sit and listen to the sounds of those who didn't need her and listlessly watch what she could see through the door of the activity she wasn't a part of. They'd been shorthanded, but they'd managed. With Moses and Daniel's help. And no need of hers.

But before she could slump in relief against her headboard, she'd need to unhitch and care for Scarlett and hobble to the house. Before that, she'd need to make her way out to the shed across the alley and hitch up the mare first. The way her ankle felt, the thought of either task, much less both, was enough to make her nauseous.

Sighing, Elizabeth closed her eyes and let her head droop against the back of the chair. At the sound of nearby footsteps, her eyes flew open and the chair creaked as she jerked upright to find herself staring into Moses's green-eyed gaze, surprising an expression on his face that was quickly disguised.

Elizabeth flushed at the look and corresponding lurch in her heart upon seeing it. This morning when she'd opened the restaurant, she hadn't thought of Moses in years, well, months at least. In the span of a few hours, he'd turned her world upside down.

But the best defense was a good offense.

"Has everyone left?" With a grunt, Elizabeth lifted her ankle off the desktop and carefully set it on the floor.

"*Ja.* Daniel is harnessing your horse."

Though she wanted to wilt with relief, Elizabeth frowned. The hands in her lap curled into fists. She'd always taken care of herself. A simple injured ankle wasn't going to change that. "How does he know which one is mine?" she challenged.

"It helps when it's the only one left in the shed."

Elizabeth used the desktop to push to her feet, fighting a grimace at the insult of gravity against her swollen ankle. The reprieve at not having to harness the mare was eking out a victory over pride—something her culture frowned on anyway—of self-sufficiency.

"Well, you might as well leave too." She lowered her brow. "Or do you want to be the last one out the door as it's yours now?"

"*Nee*, you can trundle behind with your stubbornness to close it, but I can't leave until you do."

That didn't make sense. She had the key; she could lock up. What was stopping him? Her chest swelled with resentment. Was this some new rule he was imposing? That she could no longer lock up on her own? Was he going to take that from her? Take that last look of the kitchen, with its clean, shiny surfaces and lingering aromas at the end of the day, before closing the door with the satisfaction of a job well done?

Not if she could help it.

"Why not?" At her tone, her staff would've known to duck their heads and keep out of the way.

Its inflection bounced right off Moses. "Because you're giving me and Daniel a ride."

Chapter Four

Her breath left in a gust. "I am not!" Her objection was ruined by an indignant step closer. On her aching ankle. And crumpling in front of him like overproofed dough in the oven. Elizabeth caught herself on the chair, but even hindered by its old wheels, the treasonous seat scooted out from underneath her. A strong hand shot out, stopping her fall. Unlike the chair, Moses's sudden grasp on her elbow was solid, stable. Elizabeth hissed in a breath.

If only he had been as well.

Judiciously keeping her weight off her injured leg, she straightened. And carefully lifted her arm from his grip.

The corner of his mouth tipped up at her mutinous expression. "All right. We'll give *you* a ride. In your own buggy. Because you can't even stand, much less take care of your horse. Besides, we're heading out in your direction. I'm told Samuel Schrock lives out that way. I understand he's the one to see when you need a horse."

Elizabeth froze. "Why do you need a horse?"

"Because at my age, I'm a little too old for a scooter and some distances are just too far to walk. Even in my *rumspringa* I never had a car."

The limited food Elizabeth had reminded herself to eat that day was suddenly twisting in her stomach. If Moses needed a horse, did that mean he was staying? A brief visit to Miller's Creek to inspect his new property was one thing; settling in, or an extended stay, was something else entirely. How long could she...er...the restaurant handle his presence without being affected? Elizabeth pressed her hand against her midsection, fervently hoping everything Samuel Schrock had in his barn at the moment was lame.

And if they were, by the time Elizabeth shuffled out of the office, she empathized with the creatures. Good thing tomorrow, except for attending church, would be more restful. As she braced herself on the counters to support her journey through the kitchen, she scrutinized the crowded room's condition. To her disgruntled acknowledgment, every surface was gleaming. Everything was in its place. Pristine plates were stacked above the equally pristine line waiting to be used for breakfast orders early Monday morning. Large containers of spices were neatly aligned by frequency of use on their shelf. Huge pots for cooking, their bottoms burnished, were stored upside down under the counters. Everything that she would've done was done. And done well. Totally without her.

Glancing back, she saw Moses, the dripping ice bag in one hand and her cloak, which he must've snagged from the peg on the wall, in the other, turn off the light in the office. Things that she'd neglected to collect and do. She who never forgot anything.

Her shoulders sagged. The energy, born of shock and frustration, that'd sustained her throughout the long day fizzled like the diminishing bubbles in a cooling pot. When Moses looked over and caught her eye, she gave him a barely discernible nod. It was all she could manage. When his lips lifted in return, Elizabeth glanced away. A soft clunk sounded behind her as Moses deposited the ice bag in the sink. Before she could make the final step to the door, he was there opening it wide ahead of her.

Scarlett was indeed harnessed and hitched to her buggy when Elizabeth hobbled across the alley, carefully skirting the wretched pothole and Moses's assistance. Using willpower and arms made strong over the years by lifting heavy pots and pans, she lurched into the buggy.

Moses climbed in the other side. "Want me to drive?"

Elizabeth gritted her teeth. "It's my ankle that was wrenched, not my wrist. I can manage my own horse."

Moses nodded to Daniel, who stared at them from outside the buggy. "Get in. We're going to the Schrocks'."

Daniel remained where he was. "I thought we were doing that another time."

"No time like the present." Moses tipped his head toward the other side of the front seat. "Not when we've got such an accommodating ride most of the way there."

With a dubious glance at Elizabeth's scowling silhouette, Daniel shrugged and slipped behind Moses into the back. When Elizabeth sent the eager horse down the alley before he was seated, he dropped onto the upholstered bench with a thud. The pavement fell away beneath clattering hooves as Elizabeth kept her eyes on the mare's chestnut mane, her posture as stiff as the little she contributed to the conversation.

While Moses occasionally eyed her silent profile, her restraint didn't seem to affect Daniel. Moses's younger tintype had ample comments to make—about the town, the restaurant, the customers. Although she had to admit the young man, like his father, had charm, Elizabeth's eyes narrowed when the conversation kept coming back to the restaurant's waitress. Her responses were as short as she hoped Daniel's interest in Rebecca was.

"My sisters waitress. The unmarried ones. *Daed*, you'd never mentioned that I recall. Did *Mamm* waitress as well?"

Elizabeth swallowed against a sudden ache in her throat at the young man's words. At hearing Moses referred to as *Daed*. If things had worked out differently, Daniel might've been her... It was no use thinking that way. The past couldn't be changed. It didn't matter. Still, she held her breath to better hear Moses's comment about his wife. To hear his inflection regarding the woman whom, unlike her, he'd cared enough about to ensure he married. It was a surprisingly long time in coming.

"Before we were married, she did. Along with your aunts. I don't think she minded when she quit."

"I didn't remember her ever working in the restaurants. She certainly would've been surprised at how you've expanded the business, all the way up here."

"I wouldn't have, if she were still alive." The sound of the wheels rolling over the pavement and the clip-clop of the mare's hooves made Moses's murmur almost indiscernible.

But Elizabeth heard it like a roar. Her fingers tightened on the reins. Her mouth dried up like a shallow pot of water left boiling on the burner. Moses was a widower? He was no longer married? He had no wife to return to? He was avail— *No, no, not for me.* Still, her heart beat faster as she sneaked a glance at the man beside her.

Her eyes almost popped out of her head when the next comment was spoken nearly into her ear.

"So, I understand you and my *daed* have a history." Daniel was all but leaning over the back of the buggy seat.

Elizabeth choked on her next breath. Heat rose up the back of her neck and spread out over her cheeks under the weight of both men's attention. She didn't want to talk about her and Moses's history. Especially upon discovering he was single. To do so might somehow bring history into the present. Make it more real when all Elizabeth wanted was to keep it in the long past, like a book once read, where characters or details couldn't be recalled, only the very basis of the plot. *I thought I could trust him and he left me.*

The silence in the buggy grew until it was like an additional passenger. Elizabeth moistened her lips. "Your *daed* used to live here. We knew each other. He moved away. As far as a history, there's not enough in it to cover the page of a first-year primer."

"Oh, Beth," Moses chided, shaking his head. "You know better than that. Surely our history more than covered the page."

Moses was surprised the horse didn't rear at the tensing of its driver. Elizabeth stabbed him with a look that warned against additional sharing of their past. Before he could provoke her further, they'd topped a small rise and the silhouette of a small, neat house and shed was revealed in the moonlight.

Moses remembered her place. Remembered bringing Elizabeth home from Sunday night singings. Remembered lingering on the porch or in the lamp-lit kitchen when the other two occupants in the house were asleep. Remembered driving by her place on the chance she might be outside. Remembered stolen moments at private picnics where they'd feasted on Elizabeth's *wunderbar* talents in the kitchen. Moses had many memories of courting her. More memories than he had of courting his wife.

He cocked his head, studying the woman who was ably handling the reins. He'd been courting in earnest, but had Elizabeth realized it? She'd always been dismissive of her attractions. Had always seemed a little startled at his attention. A little suspicious. A smile touched his mouth. He'd always been able to charm her out of that once they were together. A little tart. A little sweet. Maybe that was what'd intrigued him. She'd kept him on his toes. And given him a brief respite from his father's expectations.

He'd had his own dreams then. Some he'd realized. Others, *ach*. With others, he hoped to discover that dreams deferred were not dreams denied. That deferred dreams, ones that'd included the woman beside him, were now possible.

The woman whose face, even in the shadows of the buggy, was currently pale with obvious discomfort. Physical? Emotional? Both systems had suffered a shock today. Which one would recover faster? The buggy lurched as, with a wary glance his way, Elizabeth urged the mare on as if they were making the homestretch run at a racetrack. Moses braced a hand against the wall when they swung into the lane. Elizabeth swayed in his direction. Although he would've welcomed the brief contact, she managed to avoid any. Moses bit the inside of his cheek. As to which would recover faster? Elizabeth would probably be capable of running at breakneck speed before she'd ever admit she was pleased to see him again. Which would make the admission, if...when...it happened, all the sweeter.

Elizabeth drew the horse to a halt in front of the yard gate. "Scarlett won't be thrilled to go back out the lane." Her gaze flicked to the shed. "I'll watch for your return and put her up when you get back."

Before Moses could make a move to assist her, she'd slid the door open and was easing her way from the buggy. He reached over to take the reins, wincing when Elizabeth sagged at her first step away from the rig. Immediately jerking upright, she shuffled to the gate.

"What you mean is that you'll wait in the barn to make

sure you're there when we return." Elizabeth didn't deny it. With a hand on the gate for support, she made no further effort to proceed up the walk. Moses sighed. She would wait the rest of the night if need be for him to leave before she hobbled inside. Stubborn woman.

He threaded the reins through his fingers. Barely giving Daniel time to move from the back to the front seat of the buggy, Moses directed the mare not toward the shed where she wanted to go, but down the lane. The mare, like her owner, briefly fought him. She made her displeasure known through laid-back ears and a stiff, reluctant gait.

Daniel watched the horse a moment before glancing back toward the dark farmyard. "The mare reminds me of someone."

Moses grunted, his lips twitching.

"Do you know where you're going?"

"Ja."

"I thought this horse trader was someone who'd moved into the area after you'd moved away."

"I know who used to own the farm where he now lives. The location of the farm doesn't change just because the owner does."

"Huh. I'm wondering about some other changes. Tell me again why you bought a restaurant in Wisconsin and why we're doing this tonight?"

"We're doing this tonight because we have a ride most of the way there."

Daniel's narrow-eyed gaze acknowledged he'd noted the omission, though he didn't pursue it. "I know. You mentioned that. We could've gotten one later. Hired an *Englisch* driver to take us out. I'm sure they have those here in Wisconsin. We didn't have to go at—" Daniel checked the bishop-approved, at least in Ohio, cell phone that he carried "—eight fifteen in the evening, when, who knows, the man might be in bed."

The mare apparently decided to stop pouting. Her gait smoothed out. The slumbering fields beyond the ditches, some with snow still laced through them, passed by at greater speed.

"Along with her injury, Beth's had a bit of a shock today. I figured the least I could do was unharness her horse."

"Doing so for that woman won't do you any good."

"Probably not."

"She'll resent it."

"Probably."

"Is this about this *history* you two have?"

"Could be."

Daniel shook his head. "She's not anything like *Mamm*. Whatever your history was, I'd say, leave it in the past. What is that saying? 'Let sleeping dogs lie'?"

Moses sent a mild scowl in his son's direction. "I don't recall making recommendations on your love life."

Daniel slumped back against the seat in exaggerated shock. "*Gut* thing, if this is your version of a love life. I'd as soon date a…porcupine. In fact, it might be about the same thing."

Moses smiled as he turned the horse into a remembered lane. Lights still glowed in the house and, to his relief, a glimmer showed in a barn window as well. He drew the mare to a halt in front of the big white double doors. "You're just looking at the surface. The one she's allowing you to see. She's got a side that she doesn't even recognize."

"Well, if she doesn't see it either, she's in *gut* company."

Chapter Five

Moses had slowed the tired mare to a walk as they ascended the lane to keep their return as quiet as possible. Still, as he got down and unhitched the Standardbred, he was surprised when Elizabeth didn't appear on the lamp-lit porch. His surprise grew, along with a bit of concern, when he led the horse into the shed, unharnessed her, fed and watered the animal, and still there was no sign of the mare's owner.

He and the horse shared a sigh as Moses slid a brush over her sweating chestnut coat. While he carried out the familiar work, his attention shifted out the window to the shadowed house a short distance away. Too early in the spring for the insects, the only sounds drifting through the dark night were the occasional call and answer of owls along the nearby creek. It was quiet, peaceful. Moses's lips twitched as he patted the mare's hip. Quiet and peaceful were alien sensations for him. Working in a busy, crowded kitchen, where communication was vital for fast and accurate service, didn't lend to quiet and peaceful. Nor did living his earlier adult years on a main street above a restaurant. Nor later years in a house raising several children.

Moses put the brush alongside a currycomb and hoof pick on the neatly organized shelf, did a final check on the mare and exited the shed. For him, the peace and quiet were pleasant changes. Having latched the door, he leaned against its wooden boards and considered the lamp glowing from a single window across the small farmyard. For the sole inhabitant of the house, out here by herself, was it peaceful? Or just lonely?

On his occasional ventures into the dining room this afternoon, folks who'd remembered him had been eager to visit. He'd heard that Elizabeth's twin sister had married some months back. With Emma moved out, Elizabeth was left here alone. Did she miss the company? Moses rubbed a hand over his short beard. She'd never admit it if she did. Quiet and peaceful were *gut*. In fact, they could certainly grow on a fellow. But…his gaze slid from the cozy house to the woods beyond, where he detected a few sets of eyes watching him from the black depths. From there, he trailed it down the short lane to the road, a road with no other homes visible in either direction. If a woman he cared for…say one of his daughters…were living here alone, it was a mite too quiet. A tad too isolated…

His eyes narrowed on the road leading to the horse trader's place. Along with no houses, there were currently no small lights pricking the darkness to indicate a buggy was heading this way. Daniel had lingered at the Schrock farm to visit with an affable Samuel. The two young men, relatively close in age, had hit it off. Though once Daniel got on the road, he shouldn't be too long, as Samuel had rented them a good-looking animal and, for the short term, even loaned them his wife's buggy.

As he intended to stay in the area, it had dented Moses's pride no small bit not to be able to buy the horse and a buggy outright. But having purchased the Dew Drop with cash, he didn't have the thousands in funds available to buy anything else without tapping into resources from his other two operations. Maybe he shouldn't have paid cash, but that was what he'd done with all his other purchases and he wasn't about to start with credit now. On the ride back, as he'd brooded over how he'd stretched not only his finances but those of his family as well, since their livelihoods depended on his other restaurants, Moses's chest had begun to squeeze. Breath had come hard. Under his jacket, donned against the crisp early spring night, sweat had trickled down his spine.

Had he overreached? Was this the risk that brought him and, as they relied on him, his family down? For half a mile, he'd driven with one hand on the lines, the other pressed against his heart, grimacing at the pain. *What if, like my father, I die and leave Daniel such a mess that it takes him years to recover?*

Thankfully, by the time he'd reached the little farm, the pain had subsided. The weight pressing down on him like a trio of anvils had lifted fractionally and he'd been able to breathe again. He'd just work harder, ensure that the business was a success, prove that purchasing it, though it was far from his others, had been a good decision. Times had been tough before. He'd survived them. Supported his family through them. He'd do it again. Even though this time, the venture was for him, not for his *daed*, not in support of his family.

Moses pushed away from the shed door and strode across the dark farmyard toward the muted lights of the house. His footsteps on the porch's wooden boards echoed in the still night, as did the series of soft knocks on the door. Knocks that went unanswered. Furrowing his brow, Moses quietly turned the knob and peeked inside.

Across the room he could see Elizabeth in the bow-arm morris chair he remembered as her *daed*'s, her foot—with a bag of ice wrapped in a dish towel perched on top—resting on a matching ottoman. Her *kapp* was crinkled where her head leaned against the chair's upholstered back. Her capable hands lay quiescent on the chair's wooden arms. Her mouth, usually flat as a pencil or frowning like a raised umbrella, was relaxed. Soft. Vulnerable? It wasn't a word he normally would've chosen for her. But at the moment, tiptoeing across the linoleum floor to gaze down at her pale face, it was the word that came to him. His lips curving into a bemused smile, Moses took his first full breath since chest pains had besieged him on the way home.

Not so fierce now, Beth.

With a gentle finger, he traced a tender line on one of the dormant hands from her wrist to the point of her index finger, marveling that her skin, though revealing hard work and the passage of time, was still so silky. Beth's eyelids quivered, then opened to reveal brown eyes currently soft as melted chocolate. They blinked a few times in puzzlement as she met his gaze.

"Moses? You're back?" The words were as soft as her eyes.

"Just a little while ago." His chest swelled. This was the Beth he'd been hoping he'd find upon his return. He was elated to have been wrong. It was indeed her sentiment, not her ankle, that had recovered fastest.

As if his thought drew her attention to the injury, blinking a few more times, Elizabeth straightened in her chair to frown at her foot.

"I just sat down for a moment. I was going to meet you at the barn." She braced herself on the arms of the chair as if to rise.

Moses rested a hand on her shoulder. "Your mare is fed, watered and tucked away for the night. It wasn't a chore, as everything in your shed is nicely organized."

Even in the low light of the nearby lantern, he could see her cheeks grow rosy. "Taking care of her was my intention. I must've fallen asleep."

"I'm glad."

The softness disappeared from her lips as they drew into a tight line. "Well, that makes one of us. I can take care of my mare. And myself. I'm no…incapable weakling."

Elizabeth willed away the flush she knew was covering her cheeks like a toasty blanket. Moses had an unfair advantage, looking down at her the way he was. And the way he was looking…it brought back memories. It allowed trickles of hope. To her disgust, the blush, instead of abating, intensified. She swallowed, quickly bolstering against any possibilities that those trickles of hope, of anticipation, pooled into something more.

Nicely organized? Well, that was what her life had been before he'd dropped back into it. That was the way it would continue to be for the brief time he remained in it, and after his broad back disappeared down the road on whatever transportation returned him to Ohio. This time when she straightened, Moses's hand dropped away. With it, the warmth, the imagined comfort, quickly faded from the dark fabric of her dress. Elizabeth shrugged her shoulder against the palpable absence.

"You don't have to get up."

"*Ja*. I do." Ready now for the discomfort, at least the physical one, she lowered her foot to the floor, scowling at how the yarn of her hand-knitted slippers stretched to its limits to accommodate a surprising amount of swelling. If she could barely get her slippers on now, what was she going to wear for church tomorrow? She gladly latched on to the future dilemma rather than dwell on longings stirred up by the unsettling expression she'd briefly caught on Moses's face.

"I know you didn't eat much in town. Have you eaten since you got home?"

She glared at Moses, now framed in the doorway to the kitchen, the counters and table in shadows behind him. "The restaurant wasn't enough? You're taking over my own kitchen?"

"Beth, as I've discovered much of you hasn't changed over the decades, I figure you're still in the habit of keeping an assortment of baked goods somewhere in your kitchen."

Elizabeth looked at her ankle, seemingly puffed up to the size of the volleyball the *youngies* played with on Sunday afternoons. And, under the black stockings she hadn't yet had the courage to try to remove, probably as blue as the ball's stripes. Her empty stomach whined to go to the kitchen. Her expanded ankle suggested staying put. Elizabeth tested it, pressing her heel against the small braided rug under the ottoman. The suggestion became a warning.

"In the cupboard next to the stove." She stared at the ottoman's navy top as she listened to Moses's movements in her dim kitchen. Though she'd grown used to silence in the house, the muted sounds as he rooted in cupboards were surprisingly comforting.

"I used to be the one feeding you," she groused quietly.

Moses returned with a banana nut muffin on a small china plate. He set it on the chair's broad wooden arm. "I'd be happy to have you do so again."

Her lips lifted in the closest thing to a smile that they'd done that day. Years ago, she'd lov—enjoyed taking care of him. Breaking the muffin in two, she scooted half of it in his direction.

"I couldn't imagine it possible, but I think your skills in

the kitchen have improved. The wedding casserole today was *wunderbar*." Moses spoke around the bit of muffin he'd popped into his mouth. "I'll have to try that idea at my other places."

The bite Elizabeth had just taken grew instantly dry at the reminder he had other businesses. Other places. He wasn't staying. The Dew Drop wasn't that important to him. Just as she hadn't been.

"I make it from memory. The recipe isn't written down. I'm sure…Ohio has its own versions."

"*Ja*. But it won't be the same."

Her lips pressed together as she recalled the relationship they'd had, that she'd *thought* they'd had. "Things seldom are."

The slight sound from outside brought Elizabeth both relief and regret. Moses glanced out the window. "Looks like Daniel's back. Guess I'll go see what he thinks of the rented horse." Crossing to the door, he paused with his hand on the knob. "It's been a tough day for you, hasn't it, Beth."

She grimaced. "I'm sure there'll be more to come."

He returned her brief nod with a slight smile and went out the door. When it shut behind him, Elizabeth pushed abruptly to her feet and hopped to where she could watch from the window as Moses, walking at a pace much slower than she'd expected, headed toward the waiting silhouette of a horse and buggy. When he stopped and looked back, she ducked behind the window's edge, wincing at the jolt to her ankle. Only when sounds indicated the buggy was in motion did she peek back out to see it descend her lane.

Her fingers curled around the window frame. *Ja*, there'd be more tough days ahead, especially if she had to struggle so hard to reinforce her defenses against him already.

Chapter Six

"Are you feeling all right?"

Elizabeth scowled as her twin sister, Emma, settled in beside her on the wooden church bench. "Why do you say that?"

"Usually you're scurrying about directing operations and today I arrive to see you already seated and so stationary, you look like you're planted."

Elizabeth picked a solitary piece of lint from her skirt. "Why would I be directing things? It's not my house."

"That hasn't stopped you before." The tart words were delivered with a smile.

Elizabeth lifted her foot an inch from the linoleum floor. Even that small effort made her swollen ankle roar in protest. "I sprained my ankle yesterday. I didn't want everyone to see me hobble around like a horse with a hoof abscess, so I arrived early and...just sat. At least the service is in a house today and I could do so, instead of having to file in with all the other women just before the service if they'd held it in the barn."

"Ouch." Emma hummed in sympathy at the sight of the puffy lump under Elizabeth's stocking. "You might recover faster if it *was* a hoof abscess."

Elizabeth grunted in response. Her sister was probably right. And she had to recover quickly before she totally lost control over her restaurant. Her hands twisted together. Other than church, her work at the restaurant was her life. It was her identity. Without it, who was she? A deceased man's daughter? A married woman's sister? The remainder of what used to be a pair of spinster twins in the community?

Brushing the disturbing thoughts aside, she pounced on Emma's earlier comment. Yesterday, her staff had welcomed and quickly warmed up to Moses—an interloper who might upend their whole operation—with his casual management style as opposed to her more…well, directive one. The kitchen had been downright cheerful under hectic conditions. Everyone had practically chirped like a tree full of birds.

The words blurted out. "Am I really that bossy?"

"You can be." At Elizabeth's involuntary wince, Emma hastily added, "But it's always with *gut* intent." The brown eyes that matched Elizabeth's own twinkled. "And sometimes you're actually right." She shrugged. "Folks are used to it. They know you are you and they respect you for it."

Only slightly mollified, Elizabeth turned toward the door as the men, who'd been congregating in the barn before the service, arrived. Her eyes widened when Moses entered with the older men to take his seat on the opposing rows of benches. How had he discovered where church would be held this Sunday? She hadn't told him. Intentionally. Couldn't she have one day without him? Elizabeth lowered her gaze. It wouldn't be difficult to keep it downcast, as was preferred. She'd seen and heard enough of Moses yesterday. And much to her disgust, he'd filled her thoughts last night as well. And now, for three hours, anytime she looked up, he would be there.

Emma's words stayed with Elizabeth as folks dispersed from the benches following the last hymn. The comments were hardly a compliment, though she knew Emma meant no disrespect in them. She'd just been speaking with a well-loved sister's honesty. But now it was like an unreachable itch between Elizabeth's shoulders that, even though they accepted it, folks in her community thought she was bossy.

Her ankle had been impossible to hide from Ruth Schrock, today's hostess, when Elizabeth had shuffled into the house early this morning, braced on the cane her *daed* had used after he'd lost a leg to diabetes. They'd come up with a stationary job for Elizabeth to help with dinner, sitting on a stool at the counter in Ruth's large kitchen and cutting desserts. Now Elizabeth creased her forehead. Had they come up with it together, or had she told Ruth what she'd be doing? The dynamics hadn't bothered her before, but in the light of Emma's comment... Her brow cleared. *Ach*, Ruth Schrock wasn't one to take direction in her own home unless she agreed with it.

Elizabeth's position at the counter allowed her to see into the common room, which had, with an efficiency born of long practice, been quickly converted from church service to dining area. The older men, as always, were eating first. From where she perched, she could hear them visiting. She listened absently as conversations ran from the weather, to how soon they might be able to get into the fields that spring, to the merits of Percherons versus Belgian horses. When a new voice—one now fixed in her brain—joined the dialogue, she sat up straighter and tilted her ears, and surreptitiously her eyes, in that direction.

Moses's presence had generated something akin to a spring flood, with folks—men and women—flowing over to offer an enthusiastic hello or exclaim over him. Curling her lip, Elizabeth jabbed her knife through a pan of brownies as she watched the continual parade.

"That row is crooked." Cilla Reihl, her preteen great-niece via Emma's marriage last year to the girl's grandfather, pointed a finger at a recently cut line. "If I were to get one from there, I'd want it from that end." Her finger hovered a fraction of an inch above the substantially cut portions on one side of the 9x12 pan as opposed to the considerably narrower ones on the other.

Elizabeth huffed out a breath. "Didn't your new *grossmammi* ever tell you that it's rude to point?"

"I'm pointing at something, not at someone, like you keep looking at." Cilla swiveled to point in Moses's direction. "Do you like him? If you do, I can matchmake for you. I helped matchmake for my grandpa, and if I can find a match for him, I can find a match for anybody."

She looked back in time to see Elizabeth gouge a brownie in the process of slapping it on a plate. "Wow. Probably better set that piece aside. You really mutilated it. It'll taste just as good, but presentation counts for something, or so I'm told." Elizabeth gaped at the girl's back as Cilla, following her words of wisdom, whisked away from the counter bearing a loaded tray.

Elizabeth's teeth closed with a *click*. With the knife held in a fisted grasp, she made precise cuts in the next pan, this one of lemon bars. Her lips pursed like she'd had the lemon without the sugar. To her chagrin, the girl was right. Presentation did count for something. When a quick scan revealed Cilla was nowhere in sight to witness it, Elizabeth sent a scowling glance at the man in the center of hearty male laughter.

Was that why Moses had always been so popular? Because he was attractive? Not just physically, although she used to roll her eyes at how he'd always made sure his hair was trimmed and neat, the sleeves of his shirt rolled up just so and the buggy he'd obtained early in his *rumspringa* wiped free of the merest dust that dared settle on it. But personality-wise as well, with a charm that would probably prompt even the local Standardbred horses to smile and nicker, should he concentrate on the effort.

The local widows and spinsters would certainly be thrilled to hear he was available. Elizabeth's knife scraped against the bottom of the metal pan. Maybe he'd even take one of their ranks back with him to Ohio when he went if, in the limited time she hoped he was here, the restaurant left him any free time to go courting. Though adding courting to his schedule would certainly reduce the amount of time she'd have to deal with him at the restaurant. Elizabeth tried to be thrilled at the prospect, but instead, the possibility prickled like the occasional nettles that dared to grow in her garden.

If he did go courting, who would he pursue?

Elizabeth gave quick consideration to the women bustling about the kitchen and dining area as they served the district's membership. Worrying her lower lip, she slid another stack of china plates closer and dished out carefully cut portions. There were single women, mature women, who gave her a nod as she caught their eye. Women who, unlike her, would be *gut* matches for Moses in appearance and personality. Some who had even been single before he'd left for Ohio decades ago.

So why had Moses been interested in her and not them?

Was that why she'd always been suspicious of his attention to her? Why she'd tested him? It had seemed unlikely a peacock would want to partner with a Leghorn chicken. Elizabeth could understand the peacock being interested in a Plymouth Rock or even a Rhode Island Red, but a Leghorn was about as plain Jane as you could get.

And she was a Leghorn.

Not only in appearance—she was a Leghorn in temperament as well. Intelligent and active birds, they were known to be noisy and could get easily bored. But productive. Leghorns were good layers and she was certainly productive. Elizabeth stared down at the apple crumb pie in front of her. Though good layers, Leghorns were rotten mothers because they didn't sit well on the eggs. With a major pang, Elizabeth slid her knife into the pie's crust.

As a Leghorn, maybe it was a good thing after all that she hadn't had children.

But instead of satisfaction, the thought weighted her stomach as if she'd eaten the entire pie in front of her at a single setting.

"So, are you staying?"

This time, Elizabeth didn't react to the question from one of Moses's current entourage. The first fifteen times she'd heard it, she'd listened so intently she'd almost toppled off her stool. After hearing the variety of his charming and evasive responses, she'd quit listening so closely. A few had asked about his wife, and her ears had pricked up, but his answers on that topic had been vague as well. No one recognized that their questions hadn't really been answered, as he'd prevaricate with a witty story or turn the conversation back to the asker.

No wonder people flocked to him.

Not like her. She was her own little island. Although folks nodded to her and, in normal circumstances when she was on both feet, would look to her for direction, no one approached just to chat. In fact, that was one of the reasons she'd gritted her teeth and come to church today when her ankle gave her adequate reason to miss. Though some went visiting after church to those who couldn't make it to the Sunday gatherings, Elizabeth didn't want to sit at home that day, doubting anyone would come, yet glancing hopefully out the window at every sound. Only to discover at the end of the long afternoon that she'd been right.

So she'd put on the only thing she could get on her foot that morning. A slipper, black to match her stockings. And no one had noticed. Because they hadn't paid close enough attention, except for Ruth Schrock this morning, to do so.

Cilla was at her elbow, loading her empty tray with plated desserts. Before the youngster could depart again, Elizabeth cleared her throat. Even so, the words were husky and hesitant. "Do you really think it would be that hard to find a match for me?"

Tilting her head, Cilla considered her with pursed lips. "*Nee*. Like my grandpa, you're kind of like my favorite fruit."

"What's that?" Elizabeth put her knife down and gave Cilla her full attention. Maybe it wasn't as bad as she thought. There were many lovely fruits to be equated with. Strawberries, for one. Her lips lifted. That would be a nice comparison. Cheery. Heart-shaped. Even bossy women wouldn't mind being aligned with hearts. Maybe especially bossy women.

"A watermelon."

Elizabeth's shoulders wilted. A watermelon? She slid a hand down the side of her dress to where her hip extended past the edges of the stool on which she perched. A little too much evidence that she liked to bake. And liked to eat what she baked. She caught a glimpse of her legs in their black hose. Even without the swollen sprain, they weren't what could be called shapely. More…sturdy. With a sigh, Elizabeth picked her knife up and made a decisive crosscut of the pie. "A watermelon," she parroted, disheartened.

"*Ja*. Hard on the outside. But softer, even sweet, inside." Cilla gave her a toothy smile. "It's my favorite. Though it's hard to pick a good one. Some people thump on them. But until you pick it and get past the rind, you don't really know what you have." She waved a hand to the room at large. "If this was a big watermelon patch, I'd pick you."

Elizabeth was once again left gaping at the girl's back. A moment later, her lips hooked into an appreciative smile. She'd been dubious, had even tried to steer her sister away when their widowed neighbor's intentionally solitary life had suddenly been complicated by an unknown granddaughter. But Emma hadn't listened, praise be to *Gott*. Because this not-quite-child, not-quite-young-woman had surprisingly become Elizabeth's secret delight.

Maybe a watermelon fit. She'd admit to currently feeling a bit green, thinking about Moses with one of the single women in the community. And, at the way her ankle was aching, she was beginning to feel a bit green physically as well.

The counter beside her was finally empty of desserts. Swiveling on her chair, Elizabeth gazed into the common room. The *youngies* had come in to eat. With them, Daniel. Elizabeth narrowed her eyes as she considered the young man. Like his father, he drew people in. Though the young single women made a point as they executed their tasks to swing by and share a smile, his gaze followed Rebecca. And hers followed him. They never approached each other, but there probably wasn't a moment when one didn't know where the other was. Elizabeth crossed her arms over her chest. She needed to put a stop to any budding courtship. Her brow lowered. And when had the *youngies* become so blatant about their interests that she'd even notice? What happened to the youth being discreet in their romances?

Courtships in her day were kept considerably under wraps until the couple was ready to make an announcement in church that a wedding would follow a few weeks later. Decades ago when she and Moses had been walking out, they'd never approached the other in public. Only after singings would he take her home as they'd prearranged. She'd hugged the knowledge to herself, knowing the other girls were wondering why Moses never asked to take them home.

Elizabeth had thanked *Gott* numerous times that few, if any, had known she and Moses had been seeing each other. She was most thankful no one had known he'd asked her to marry and leave with him and his family for Ohio. Though her heart had been almost leaping from her chest with the desire to shriek yes, Elizabeth had turned him down, using the legitimate reason of her *daed*'s illness as an excuse. What if Moses hadn't really been serious—a peacock and a Leghorn together? What if he'd been mocking her?

When he'd left and she'd never heard from him again, she knew he hadn't been serious. If he had, he wouldn't have given up so easily. He'd been toying with her. So it was a *gut* thing she'd tested him, a test which he'd failed. But as his laughter drifted from the far corner of the room, Elizabeth grimaced. It didn't feel like such a particularly *gut* thing right now.

She eased herself off the stool, wincing when her foot touched the floor and jarred her swollen ankle. The day's activities had taken a toll on the joint. It was hot. Irritated. Her stubbornness had taken a toll on it. She should've stayed home. Elizabeth grabbed the cane she'd hooked on one of the rungs. With one last look in Moses's direction, she left the kitchen as quietly as she could.

Her stubbornness had taken a toll on a number of things in her life.

Chapter Seven

E lizabeth slowed Scarlett to a walk, the clip-clop of the mare's shod hooves the only sound echoing through the alley behind the restaurant the next morning. Peering through the four o'clock darkness, Elizabeth guided the Standardbred around the black pit of the pothole. It was bad enough she was limping; she didn't need Scarlett to be as well. Drawing the horse to a halt, Elizabeth sighed as she eyed the restaurant's dark shape in the row of silent buildings that lined the alley. She'd never had problems waking in what some would consider the middle of the night. Today, other than the first tentative touch to the floor to confirm that, *ja*, her ankle was still very unhappy, she'd been eager to be up, eager for an hour of quiet baking before more staff arrived. Before *he* arrived. Eager for a moment of peace inside her kitchen. Peace she hadn't experienced since Rebecca had mentioned scrapple.

Peace that was shattered when the mare's quiet nicker was returned by another horse. With a gasp, Elizabeth jerked her head toward the shadows of the low-slung shed where an unseen occupant rustled.

Surely Moses wasn't here already?

Elizabeth firmed her lips when she found herself smiling. She shouldn't be excited. Moses being here already would be terrible. She'd been anticipating a quiet hour to herself, an hour without his unwanted company, without his presence in her restaurant and therefore in her life. Still, as she set the buggy's brake and climbed down, her heart was pounding much faster than the simple action required. Her eyes flicked from the silhouette of a buggy's shaft peeking out beyond the horse shed to the back door of the restaurant.

The unseen horse nickered again. Ignoring the request for Scarlett to join it, Elizabeth limped across the alley to the back door. Would Moses know what to start first to ensure everything was ready for their early morning customers? Was he rearranging her kitchen when she wasn't there? She huffed in a breath. How would she find anything? Her gait quickened as disdained excitement made way for growing indignation.

Ready to chastise Moses, whatever he was doing, Elizabeth tugged on the doorknob. It didn't move. Frowning at the delay, she dug out her key and inserted it in the lock. Whereas she, as did most Amish she knew, left her rural home unlocked, an *Englisch* business in town was different. When the lock went *click*, Elizabeth jerked the door open. To pitch blackness.

Her shoulders sagged. With a long sigh, she reached in and flicked on the lights to peer into the empty kitchen. He obviously wasn't there. She should be thrilled. Why, then, did her enthusiasm for the day suddenly dim? The door clanged shut behind her as she shuffled back to where Scarlett waited, slump-hipped, to be unhitched and unharnessed.

"What are you doing here?"

Elizabeth's heart catapulted into her throat when the voice erupted from the dark alley. She stumbled, jarring her ankle and barely biting off a shriek at the resultant pain. Hopping the last few feet to the buggy, she leaned against a wooden wheel and glared at Moses, who'd materialized from the gloom farther up the narrow passage.

"It should be obvious. I'm coming in to work."

When Moses reached her, the dark brim of his hat dipped as he glanced to where, beneath the hem of her skirt, she stood on one foot. "Not today."

Elizabeth's sharp inhalation bounced off the row of buildings that lined the alley.

"Good thing it's too early in the year for flies, Beth, or your gaping mouth would certainly catch them. Go home. You've got a slipper on. You're not even wearing a shoe. Come back on the day you can get a shoe on. On without prying your foot into it."

"I'll be fine." Elizabeth gritted out the words.

"*Fine*, like the white-faced *fine* you were yesterday when you could hardly make it out of the Schrocks' kitchen? That kind of fine? You're not staying today. You're supposed to be taking care of that ankle. Ice. Compression. Elevation. *Rest.* All of which are missing."

Elizabeth crossed her arms over her chest. What happened to the Moses Glick charm she'd complained about yesterday? Or was it reserved for everyone but her? "I can manage."

"Not today, you can't." Moses sighed. "Beth, go home and rest." When she returned his look with a stubborn stare, he jerked his hat off and shoved a hand through his hair. "Go home, Beth, or you're fired."

Elizabeth's head whirled at his words. She slumped against the wheel. Moses took a quick step toward her. When she shied away from his outstretched hand, he slowly dropped it.

"I don't want to do it. But if you're not going to take care of yourself, someone else needs to. Go home, elevate that ankle, and rest." Moses tugged his hat back over his hair.

Just what she'd been afraid of. He'd been waiting for

an opportunity to get rid of her. Elizabeth bit down on her trembling lip. Her nose prickled with the horrific threat of tears. Opening her mouth to speak, she had to swallow twice before she could do so. She couldn't claim he couldn't fire her, because he could.

"What about breakfast preparations? You don't know what to do."

His hat's brim shadowed his eyes, but for the first time since he'd startled her in the alley, instead of being as tight as hers, Moses's lips twitched. "I'll look at the menu and see what needs to be done." He lifted his hands. "I'll run a special. Beth, decades ago, our business in Ohio started with a bakery. I'll figure something out for breakfast. It will be all right. Get your ankle well so you can argue with me standing on two feet. Otherwise you give me an advantage. And I know that's the last thing you want to do."

She would not succumb to the flash of white teeth in his crooked smile. Shoving away from the wagon wheel so abruptly she picked up a splinter, Elizabeth climbed up the buggy steps. Heat rose up the back of her neck at the knowledge Moses was watching her awkward scramble.

Guiding a confused Scarlett down the alley, Elizabeth didn't look back as she turned onto the deserted street. Well, he better learn how to handle breakfast. Because she was going to save him the bother of firing her. She'd quit.

Moses's gaze followed the buggy, the orange slow-moving-vehicle triangle and the district-approved battery lights marking its progress down the alley and out onto the street. Only when it was completely out of sight and obviously wasn't turning around did he pivot toward the shed where the gelding impatiently rustled inside. As Daniel and he were staying in a small apartment above a quilt shop a block or so down the street, Moses figured the restaurant's shed was as good a place as any to stable the rented horse.

"Sorry to chase away your company, boy. But it pained me yesterday to watch that stubborn woman at church, knowing how much she must be hurting. I needed to do something to get her attention. For sure and certain, you can catch more flies with honey than you can with vinegar. I didn't want to threaten her job. Just between you and me, I'd never fire her. But sometimes, if honey isn't working, you need to remind the flies that vinegar exists so they remember they prefer the honey." Moses patted the gelding's dark hip. Since he was there, he measured out some feed for the appreciative horse and filled and rehung the hay net.

"Maybe I was wrong. Maybe I made a mistake. You'd think that with as many sisters and daughters as I have, I'd know how to handle women. At least, *I* thought so. Even prickly ones. I thought I used to know how to handle her. Although 'handling' is an inaccurate term. You don't 'handle' a woman. You understand her. Accept her. Support her." Moses grabbed the pitchfork and did a quick cleanup of the stall. After depositing the refuse in the indicated bin at the back of the shed, he leaned on the wooden handle as he listened to the *crunch, crunch* of the gelding eating.

You love her. Moses rubbed a hand over his mouth. Years ago, he was sure he had. So certain, in fact, he'd returned to Wisconsin because of it. He'd expected prickly. Anticipated it. But what he'd been receiving would make a cranky porcupine look cuddly. Maybe you could never go home again. Could never go back. After over two decades of responsibility, was he trying to re-create the freedom of his youth in some way?

He didn't think so. Surely he hadn't been imagining what Beth and he had together. Something he'd never been able to attain with his wife, though she'd been a *gut* and loving woman.

But if Beth was prickly, she'd be even more so if word got out breakfast preparations weren't well on their way when the other staff came in. Or if customers weren't entirely satisfied with what he accomplished in the next few hours. And if she heard about it, then he'd hear about it. The thought brought a smile to his face. Prickly though she may be, Beth was never boring. After returning the pitchfork to its twin pegs on the wall, Moses gave the horse a final pat.

"Thanks for being a *gut* listener. I imagine before Beth and I get settled, I'll need a few more conversations."

He then headed across the alley to the restaurant. Once inside, Moses glanced toward the silent kitchen as he ducked into the small bathroom to scrub his hands. He needed to get things started, but the time alone gave him a chance to examine his new purchase more closely. Something he'd intended to do Saturday night before determining that seeing Beth home took precedence. His eyes narrowed on the shiny surfaces. Though sparkling clean, the restaurant's equipment was a lot older, a lot more worn than he'd expected.

What else was not as he'd expected? He needed to look at the records. Review vendor prices. Compare them to what he was paying the vendors he used in Ohio. Were there opportunities to save money with a switch? Or at least coax a higher-priced vendor to match a lower price? When were the last health and fire inspection visits? How had the restaurant rated? What areas, if any, needed work? Were inspections in Wisconsin annual or semiannual? Were they getting close to another unannounced visit? He didn't expect there to be any issues. Beth had an eye for details and was surely a competent manager.

Moses paused by one of the biggest appliances in the

kitchen, a combination grill and gas stovetop. He'd taken a turn on the grill Saturday and had been glad to note the ventilation hood had recently been cleaned. Grills in restaurants generated a lot of grease and could be a fire hazard if not cleaned frequently. Not just the interior and exterior of the hood, but the traps and filters as well. This hood was kept in good order, but it was older, much older, than he'd expected. In fact, Moses was surprised it met fire suppression standards. Were the standards in Wisconsin different from Ohio? This one must've passed code, as they were cooking under it. Still, it was something he'd want to upgrade as soon as possible. But with the thousands of dollars in unexpected costs required to do so, it wouldn't be right away.

His stomach clenched. Had he made a mistake in buying the Dew Drop? He'd threatened to fire Beth today. Not the direction he'd hoped their relationship would go. Had he made a mistake in coming back at all?

Elizabeth slipped the needle through the fabric, through long practice hooking the backing before bringing it up through batting to reappear on the quilt top. Her stitches were neat and even. Unlike her initial stitches when she'd returned home that morning. Those had been erratic, driven by agitated fingers.

By noon, her ankle, after hours of elevation and rest, no longer ached. The yarn at the top of her slipper wasn't quite so stretched and no longer dug into her flesh. Maybe she *had* been pushing the limb a little too hard. Nothing she'd ever admit to Moses, of course. Although she might inform him the day at home was pleasant, because it gave her a day away from him.

Elizabeth debated pulling out the erratic stitches, but

decided against it. Just as she'd decided against ideas she'd
muttered to herself throughout the morning. Like quitting.
Not only quitting, but using her savings to buy another
restaurant. Not only buying another restaurant, but taking
all the Dew Drop's staff—*her* staff—along with her. Not
only setting up another restaurant, but driving Moses out
of business with her competition.

The problem was, she didn't know of any restaurants for
sale within buggy distance. And her staff might not want
to leave with her. And she really didn't want to drive the
Dew Drop out of business. After more than twenty years,
it was her home. She wanted to run it. Own it.

And something else she had to own: during moments
with Moses, she felt more alive than she had in months.
In years.

By early afternoon, she pushed the unfinished quilt off
her lap. The house was so quiet. That was *gut*, wasn't it?
If she was a bit peevish, it wasn't because it was too quiet,
or that she was lonely. She was just so used to the bustle
of the restaurant. The continuous activity. The feeling of
productivity. She wasn't grumpy because Moses was at the
Dew Drop charming everyone else in the kitchen. In the
restaurant. Probably in the whole town, if not the county.
While she was here at home. By herself.

Elizabeth leaned her head back against the cushion of the
morris chair, only to jerk forward at the clatter of hooves
coming up the lane. Was it Moses? She swung her foot from
the ottoman and levered herself from her chair. Using the
cane hooked on the wooden arm, she eagerly limped toward the window. Halfway across the linoleum floor, she
paused. So what if it was Moses? Was she to have no peace?
Couldn't he leave her alone for even one day?

Still, she ran damp palms down the front of her apron before shuffling at a more measured pace to the door. Maybe he was here because he wasn't able to manage the restaurant without her today? The corners of her mouth curled up at the prospect.

But if she wasn't at work, well, for sure and certain, he should be. He was now the owner, as he liked to remind her. A manager should be there. When she pointed that out, she'd conveniently omit that, in the past months since the *Englisch* owners had moved out of state, on the rare days off she took, there essentially hadn't been a manager on-site. The team all knew what to do, and if there were any issues, Rebecca, a capable and long-term employee, was in charge.

Why are you smiling, Elizabeth? The man threatened to fire you today. With no job, and no purpose, what then is your value? He took away your hopes before. Now he could obliterate your livelihood as well as your dreams. Remember that. Grabbing a sweater from the back of a chair, Elizabeth schooled her features into a bland expression, opened the door and, keeping her limp to a minimum, stepped out onto the porch.

"What are you doing here? Can't you leave someone alone? Particularly someone you threatened to fire today? Shouldn't you be at *your* restaurant?"

"I figured you were missing me." Moses, after a quick glance at where she stood on both feet, grinned as he climbed down from the buggy.

Though delight blossomed within her, Elizabeth propped her hands on her hips. "Not hardly. I managed fine without you for a few decades. I was actually relishing being away from you."

Anticipating his retort, she furrowed her brow when, instead of mounting the steps as she'd expected, Moses turned back to the buggy. Sliding the door open a little farther, he gathered something into his arms and lifted it out.

Elizabeth's arms dropped to her sides and she jerked back against the door as he set it on the ground. "What is that?"

Brushing his hands off, Moses glanced at the creature beside him. "Well, in Ohio, they call it a dog. Maybe it's a *gut* thing I bought the Dew Drop. You're spending too much time in the restaurant if you can't recognize one anymore."

Pressed against the door, Elizabeth buried her clenched fist in the folds of her skirt. She was surprised Moses couldn't hear her pounding heart from where he stood. "I know it's a dog. I mean, what is it doing here?"

"I'm hoping it can live here."

Elizabeth's gaze darted from the gray-muzzled black dog, which was looking dubiously around, to Moses and back again. "That's a ridiculous notion." At her sharp tone, the dog's gently wagging tail slowed to a stop.

Moses's shoulders rose and fell on a heavy sigh. "*Ach*, that's too bad. She doesn't have any place, then." He leaned to pat the knee-high dog between its V-shaped ears. "Sorry, old girl. I was hoping you two could work something out. Looks like I was wrong. I guess it's off to the pound for you."

The dog looked up at him with solemn brown eyes. Elizabeth crossed her arms over her chest. "What do you mean she doesn't have a place?"

Moses continued to run his fingers over the sleek black head. "I went into the dining area to check on things after the breakfast rush this morning. I got to visiting with a couple of *Englisch* men in one of the booths. They were lamenting about an aunt who could no longer care for herself and was going into some *Englisch* care facility."

Elizabeth grunted. The Amish had a cradle-to-grave society, where elderly family members were taken care of in the home or, if they preferred more independence, in a *daadi haus* attached to or nearby the primary home. In fact, helping take care of her ailing father through his decline in health was the reason she'd given Moses for her refusal when he'd asked her to marry him. But she knew the elderly remaining in the house wasn't always the case with the *Englisch.*

"What does that have to do with the dog?"

"It's her dog. The facility doesn't accept pets, and due to a variety of reasons—allergies, lack of space, too many other pets already, and so forth—the rest of the family can't accept their aunt's dog either. So, though it disturbs them, poor Onyx here is facing an uncertain future. Due to her age, the *Englischers* doubt she'd get adopted."

Lowering herself to the ground, the dog rested her muzzle on outstretched front legs and turned a long-suffering gaze to Elizabeth. The dog obviously realized the outcome wasn't going to be in her favor.

Elizabeth opened her mouth to tell Moses to put the creature back in the buggy and leave, but the words wouldn't form. Closing her mouth, she swallowed. The dog's future, or lack of it, wasn't her problem. Clamping her arms more tightly about herself, she frowned and swallowed again. It would be unthinkable for her to take a dog, of all things. The dog returned her look as if she understood her dilemma. And forgave her. Her tail swished slowly across the gravel. She didn't look threatening. She looked…forbearing. Resigned. What changes had the creature recently endured? The dog had no control over her future. Even with the unexpected sale of the restaurant, at least Elizabeth had her home.

"Why would you think the two of us could work something out?" *That wasn't what I'd been intending to say.*

Moses ran a hand through his short beard. "I was thinking she could be company for you."

Elizabeth scowled at him before returning her attention to the dog. "Why would I need company?"

"I noticed the other day how quiet it was out here. Quiet is nice, but it's also nice to have some type of alert system. I'd heard tell about that *Englisch* car gang one of the local boys was tangled up in over a year or so ago and thought it might be nice for you to have something that would alert you to…company."

Maybe so. But not a dog. Elizabeth tugged at her bottom lip. "I was thinking about getting a cat."

"Oh, *ja*. A cat would be pretty intimidating for a stranger. I know I'd retreat if I heard one meowing on the other side of a door." Moses shook his head. "You don't need a cat, Beth. You need something that will take direction from you. Not the other way around."

"She doesn't look intimidating." *To anyone except me.*

Moses considered the dog at his feet. "I might have to agree with you there. But she needs a home, Beth. The situation might not help you, but it would help the dog. I can't keep her in my rented space with the hours I'll be working, or I would. Her world has been turned upside down. She hasn't a place to go."

Elizabeth rubbed a hand across the back of her neck as she stared at the dog. A creature who no longer had any home. Or purpose. As if feeling her attention, the old girl sighed.

"It can't come in the house. It'll have to stay outside. I won't have it in the house."

"I think, given the alternative, she'll agree to that."

"And it's only for tonight. Or until you find other arrangements. Dogs…um… I can't keep a dog."

Moses squatted next to the prone animal and ran a hand

down her back. "What do you think, Onyx? Does this nice covered porch sound better than going to a pound?"

The dog sat up. Her mouth opened in a semblance of a smile as she panted lightly. Elizabeth hissed in a quiet breath at the abundance of teeth.

"The *Englischers* sent along some supplies just in case something could be worked out." Moses leaned into the buggy to pull out a big bag of dog food and an old blanket. "Her food dish is in the bag along with her toy."

Elizabeth retreated as Moses, followed by the dog, carried the items up the porch steps. "Where do you want them?" With a tight frown, Elizabeth gestured to the opposite side of the porch. Moses set the bag down against the wall and straightened the blanket on the wooden floor next to it.

"Ankle better?"

"You're asking now? After you bring me a creature to take care of?"

Moses smiled. "Only because I have great confidence in you, Beth." His gaze traveled over the wide porch between her and the dog. He rubbed his hands together. "Well, as you mentioned, I do need to get back to the restaurant before the supper rush. I'll leave you two to get acquainted, then." He stopped to give the dog a final pat. The dog's dark brown eyes directed a doubtful expression his way. Moses's lips twitched. "Be patient with her. Bide your time and I think you'll be in for a pleasant surprise."

Elizabeth didn't know if the murmur was intended for her or the dog.

With a final wave, Moses descended the steps and climbed into the buggy. A moment later, he was headed down the lane. Leaving her alone. With a dog.

Elizabeth, her arms wrapped tightly about herself, cleared her throat. "So… Onyx, is it?" From the far side of the porch, the dog gave a tentative wag of her tail. "We'll see how this goes. But don't expect much." Elizabeth's gaze followed the buggy as it sped down the road. "He's hard to turn down. I did it once." She sighed. "I've regretted that. Maybe that's why you're here right now. But don't get too comfortable. It's only for a short time."

With a wary eye on the dog, Elizabeth edged close enough to unroll the top of the big double-lined paper bag. She wrinkled her nose at the smell wafting from the small brown chunks that nearly filled it, leaving only room for a couple of dishes and a toy rubber duck. When Onyx moved a step closer, Elizabeth shrank back.

"Stay there." She pointed.

Unoffended, the animal sat patiently as Elizabeth set one bowl on the floor and, after a moment's hesitation, dipped the other into the chunks and set it beside the first.

"Here's this." She tossed the rubber duck toward the dog, who gently scooped it into her mouth. "I suppose the other bowl is for water. If you just stay back there, I'll get you some."

Rubber duck in her mouth, the dog seemed content to lie down and wait.

Although both dark in color, there was nothing similar in manner between this dog and the one in her past. Elizabeth couldn't have said what color that one had actually been. All she remembered was that it was dark. And big. Although big was relative to a six-year-old.

Big was apparently relative to her father as well. From the day they were born, Elizabeth had always been larger than Emma. As a widowed man with twin little girls he didn't know what to do with, he'd latched on to Elizabeth's larger size as indication she was somehow older than the petite Emma. "Take care of your little sister, Elizabeth," he'd admonish as he headed out to the fields.

And Elizabeth had. Or tried to. When they started school at age six, it was Elizabeth who, after they'd cleaned up breakfast, ensured they had their lunches packed and were out the door in time. Elizabeth who led the two-mile walk to the nearest schoolhouse.

It was Elizabeth who was leading the way home that winter day when the dog was out in the *Englisch* yard. A big dark dog, which had stood at the end of the lane, head lowered, hackles raised. Elizabeth hadn't noticed it until she'd almost been upon it. Trudging along the snow-covered road, she'd been wishing she had a best friend like Emma did. Even now, her twin was following a short distance behind, her head bent with Priscilla's as they chattered over the day's activities.

Elizabeth had been looking back at them when she'd heard the growl. Guttural, menacing, the sound had sent chills up her spine. She'd skidded to a halt on the slippery blacktop.

Moments passed while she and the dog stared at each other across the short distance. When she could hear Emma and Priscilla visiting behind her, Elizabeth finally found her voice.

"Emma. Go walk on the other side of the road," she'd called without breaking eye contact with the dog. After a few seconds, light footsteps crunching in the unplowed snow on the far side of the road indicated her twin had followed her instructions. Elizabeth could see their black cloaks in her peripheral vision. The dog noticed them as well. With a show of teeth, he slunk in their direction.

"Hey!" Elizabeth moved a few steps closer. The dog

whipped his head back toward her. The other girls, with anxious looks at the beast, hurried on.

"Don't run! It might chase you."

Heeding Elizabeth's advice, Emma and Priscilla slowed to a fast walk, their faces white under their black bonnets. Elizabeth released a small sigh when they dropped out of sight over a small hill. Now it was only her.

Mouth dry, eyes still on the dog, she inched toward the far side of the road. The dog watched her every move. When she drew parallel with him, he snarled and lunged with snapping teeth. She jerked back. But not before the dog latched on to her arm through the folds of her cloak. Even now, Elizabeth cringed as if she could still hear the throaty growl as the dog tried to tug her off her feet.

Trying to stay upright, she opened her mouth to scream. Before she could get a sound out, missiles struck the beast. With a grunt, he released her and turned to the new threat. Yards away, Thomas Reihl was scooping up snow from the side of the road for another foray.

"Git!" He pelted the dog again. With a small yelp, the dog ran into his yard, only stopping to look back once he mounted the front steps of the house.

"You all right?"

Elizabeth nodded a trembling chin as she plucked her torn cloak away from her smarting arm. She didn't wait for Thomas to catch up to her. Just went skidding up the road after her sister. She slowed down before she caught up with Emma and Priscilla, who both looked back and smiled with relief when they saw her.

When they reached their farm, Elizabeth went into the house, leaving the two other girls to linger on the road with their farewells as Thomas caught up with them. Once inside, Elizabeth had rushed to the bathroom to inspect her wounds. Though she'd mourned the holes in her only cloak, she was thankful the garment had bunched in the dog's mouth, protecting her from the worst of the bite. She'd cleaned and treated the bite with iodine. For the next few weeks, she'd worn a sweater until the marks healed and had mended the tears in her cloak when no one was watching.

After that, they went a different way to school, even though it added a half mile to the route. Emma had never spoken of the incident. Her father had never noticed. And Elizabeth had been petrified of dogs ever since.

Elizabeth hobbled back outside and, with a wary eye on the elderly dog, set the filled bowl of water down next to the food dish before retreating behind the screen door. The dog lurched to her feet. Carefully setting down the duck, she ambled over to the food. Instead of eating, she cocked her head in Elizabeth's direction.

"That's all you're going to get. I don't have anything else for you. It's supposed to be a decent night tonight, so you should be all right with just your blanket." Elizabeth looked beyond the porch to the unfenced yard. "If you leave, I blame you. This probably won't work out. But if you do happen to stay tonight, like I said, don't expect too much."

When the dog continued to watch her, Elizabeth gestured toward the bowl. At the motion, the dog dropped her head to politely eat, checking the screen door after every mouthful. Elizabeth sighed as she considered the bits of snow still lining the yard from where the biggest drifts hadn't fully melted. She cracked the door open and shuffled back outside. "You just stay over there. I've got to take care of the horse anyway. I suppose I could set you up something in the shed and leave the door open. But this is only for tonight."

Keeping a watchful eye on the feeding dog, Elizabeth

made her way down the steps with the cane. "Only Moses would threaten to fire me this morning and bring me a dog this afternoon." *Why would I have ever cared for a man who would do such a thing?*

Chapter Eight

Though he didn't look over from where he was rolling out dough, Moses smiled at the creak of the restaurant's alley door. *You better be in a shoe, Beth. If not, I'm sending you home again.* He listened to her determined, but still uneven, gait. When she rounded the corner, he stepped back and pointedly glanced at her feet.

"It's a shoe. It's on," she countered when he lifted an eyebrow.

"Barely." Only the tips of the shoe's laces remained under a tiny bow. The rest stretched over the black shoe's tongue like a corset on a whale. "Can you stand without hurting?"

Beth briefly glowered at him before her gaze slid away.

"*Gut* thing that I set something up for you, then." Moses pulled two stools, one taller than the other, from under the counter. "Why don't you take over on the dough."

Her lips twitched, but after stopping in the bathroom to wash her hands, she limped over to take a seat on one stool and lifted her foot to the other once she'd adjusted its location.

Ja, Beth, you keep that smile hidden. I know it's going to break through sometime. It's hard to believe, but your face won't crack when it does. Moses retrieved peppers from the cooler and began to slice and remove their seeds. "How's Onyx?"

Beth snorted. "She's still there." Before she could climb from her perch, Moses set a container of melted butter and one of a sugar-and-cinnamon mix on the floured counter. Beth looked from him to the containers and scowled. "When are you going to find her another place? A permanent one."

"I'll look." Moses deftly diced the peppers and slid them into a waiting bowl. *But not too hard.*

"Any complaints yesterday?"

Careful there, Beth. You almost sound hopeful. "Not with you gone." He looked up in time to catch a fluttering smile before it was wrestled back into a thin flat line. He switched to chopping onions. Even their pungent odor couldn't dim his own grin.

Elizabeth rolled the butter and sugar-spice coated dough into a long cylinder. "Did you mess with my menu yesterday?"

"Your menu survived. And so did everyone else." Along with a greased pan, he added a package of dental floss to her counter.

"Huh." Having extracted a length of floss, Elizabeth used it to slice the dough before placing the cut rolls into the pan.

They worked in companionable silence for a while. When the back door clanged, they both looked over to see Daniel step into the kitchen. Following a jaw-cracking yawn, he took off his hat, traded it for a hairnet from a box on a shelf and slipped it over his bowl-cut locks. "What do you need?" When his gaze touched on Elizabeth, he frowned.

"You can finish the prep for the omelets. I'll get started on the gravy. Beth, you ready to start the biscuits?"

At her nod, Moses slid a trash can beside her. While she scraped the remaining residue from the sweet rolls into it and cleaned the surface of the counter, he collected the ingredients for biscuits and set them next to an industrial-size mixing bowl.

After scooting her stool over to that location, Elizabeth measured ingredients into the mixer. By the time Rebecca arrived, breakfast preparations were well in hand. *Gut* thing, as his son was distracted from the moment the young woman walked into the kitchen.

"Are we ready out there?" Moses nodded toward the swinging door into the still-dark dining room.

"I'd assume so, but I wasn't on yesterday. I'll check."

"I'll give her a hand." Daniel hastened to the door after the waitress.

"It doesn't take both of you to turn on the lights. If she needs you, she has a voice. She'll call." Elizabeth's voice carried across the kitchen.

Daniel speared him with a look. Moses sighed. "Check to make sure all the menus have been wiped down and the napkin holders are full." As his son disappeared through the swinging door, Beth rolled her eyes and opened her mouth. Presumably to disagree.

A diversion was as good a defense as any. "When was the last health inspection? Are we due for one soon? How did the Dew Drop fare? Anything we needed to correct after the last one?"

It worked. She blinked. "I don't know. The previous owners always took care of that."

Moses's brows furrowed. The health inspector visits were unannounced. "You were never here during the inspections?"

"I probably was, but I didn't go around with them. The owners always did. But the reports should be on file in there somewhere." She tipped her head toward the cubby-hole office.

"Hmm. I'll look them up after the breakfast rush." Pausing beside the stove hood that hovered over the stove and grill, he added, "And the latest fire inspection."

The back door banged, and Wally, the dishwasher, and Sadie, another cook, appeared around the corner. Their nods of greeting were accompanied by yawns as they put up their coats and shuffled to their workstations. Moses smiled. Being at work while the rest of the county was just rolling out of bed took a special kind of person.

Elizabeth slid from her stool and hobbled over to the swinging door into the dining room. "As you're out there, you might as well unlock and flip the sign to Open," she hollered. "Do we still have one waitstaff on this shift, or did two suddenly become required?"

A minute later, a red-faced Daniel pushed through the swinging door. "Door is unlocked," he muttered as he took position at the grill.

Rebecca followed shortly after, the pink in her cheeks advertising her own sheepishness. "I'll fill the soda dispenser." Grabbing a small clean bucket, she lifted the lid of the silver ice machine. All heads turned in her direction when it dropped with a bang. "There's no ice."

Daniel was at her elbow in an instant. He lifted the lid and peered inside. "We've got a problem, *Daed*. Was it working last night?"

Moses's stomach knotted. Ice was vital for a restaurant. He hurried over to inspect the cavernous bin of the old machine. Only a handful of melting ice cubes were scattered over its water-laden bottom. Ominously, the machine was as quiet as the watching occupants of the kitchen. "I thought so. Check the bin of the soda dispenser."

Daniel lifted the large lid above the nozzles and chute that, along with ice, delivered various kinds of soda. "A third. Maybe a little less."

A relief, but only a temporary one. The ice in the dispenser's bin not only cooled a drink in a glass but, more critically, chilled the cold plate that the carbonated water and syrup lines ran through. Without ice covering the cold plate, the soda didn't stay carbonated. Customers didn't like flat sodas.

"Wally? Do you have a car?"

The *Englisch* teenager looked up from where he'd started washing measuring cups and bowls. "Yah."

"I'll get you some cash. We need ice. Run down to the Piggly Wiggly and pick up bags of that and a few bottles of soda. Rebecca can tell you the more popular flavors."

Wally eyed the clock as he dried his hands. "It's kind of early. Is the grocery store open yet?"

Moses blew out a breath. "I hope so. *Ach*, if not, I guess you'll be ready at the door when it does."

Rebecca set the bucket down. "What do I do if someone wants soda in the meantime?"

Elizabeth scowled. "The Pig opens at the same time we do. And who would drink sodas at breakfast?"

"Hard to tell anymore, but either way, we should be good for a short while. *Gut* thing it's spring and chilly enough folks generally prefer coffee. Rebecca, if the ice runs out and someone wants a soda before Wally gets back, offer them orange juice or milk free of charge. Beth, who do you usually call for repairs? Someone quick about responding, I hope."

Beth furrowed her brow. "Aaron Raber. He's usually pretty *gut*. He doesn't do a lot of this kind of thing, but he works with refrigerators and such."

Moses rubbed a hand over the back of his neck. Hopefully the repairman had enough experience with "and such" that he'd quickly recognize the issue with the ice maker.

Having the parts to fix it would be another matter. His stomach churned as he eyed the old machine. Could it even be fixed? His Ohio restaurants had ice makers newer than this when he'd bought the operations, so he didn't know what it would cost to replace it, but a commercial one wouldn't be cheap. Whatever the cost was, given his current finances, it was too high.

"All right. Just because we may have a bit of trouble with some beverages doesn't change the fact that folks come in for the food. So let's make sure we take *gut* care of them on that." He retrieved some bills and handed them to Wally. "Don't speed. But hurry back."

The youth took him at his word. Thirty minutes later the teenager reentered the alley door, weighted down with bags of ice and soda bottles. "There's more in my car." He set the bags down and headed back out.

"*Gut* thing. The repairman won't be able to get here until this afternoon. Depending on what he finds, we might need to send you on another trip." Moses deposited enough ice into the soda dispenser to fill it and took the remaining bags into the walk-in freezer.

Throughout the busy breakfast hours, he kept darting glances at the silent ice maker, as if it was some creature that would bite him if he wasn't wary. Which it just might do if the repairman couldn't give him some good news when he finally arrived.

Elizabeth knew she could've handled the minor crisis, but she was mildly surprised at her relief she didn't have to. She was more than mildly relieved that her ankle, though achy, didn't give her any more problems than it did. Her lips twisted. Something she probably owed to Moses and the stool he'd acquired from somewhere, which allowed her to keep her foot elevated a good share of the busy morning while others flowed about her like she was a rock in the middle of a fast-moving stream. *Ach*, she might be a rock in the stream, but at least she was in the water today.

The first rush of the day over, Moses was in her office, rooting through drawers. Elizabeth tapped a finger against her pursed lips as she tried to work up agitation that he was going through the files in her desk. There was surprisingly little to dredge up. Paperwork was far from her favorite part of the operation. She loved to bake, to cook, to plan meals and acquire the ingredients to do so. She enjoyed feeding a large number of folks in an energized environment with good teammates, ones she'd hired and trained.

She didn't care for the regulatory aspect of restaurant management. The government paperwork and such. Fortunately, the previous owners had taken the required courses and had addressed that. If there were things she'd needed to undertake when they'd moved out of state, she figured they would've advised her when and what needed to be done. Her mouth curled at the corners as her gaze lingered on the man seated on the edge of the office chair while his fingers rifled through hanging files in an open drawer. If Moses wanted to take over those tasks, well, she'd let him.

Elizabeth lifted her head at a muted thumping noise before shifting to scan the kitchen for its source. *Thump, thump, thump.* Her brows lowered. Where was it coming from? Sliding off her stool, she limped toward the walk-in cooler, reaching it just as the heavy door burst open and Rebecca, a gallon jug of orange juice in one hand, tumbled out.

"Whoa! That gave me a bit of a fright." The waitress pressed a hand to her chest. "I thought you were going to find me chilled next to the cottage cheese by lunchtime." She rattled the handle that extended through the thick door via a lengthy, heavy bolt before shutting the door with a robust *click*. "The handle is loose. I couldn't get it open at first." Shuddering, she blew out a breath before lifting the jug of juice. "The one in the refrigerator was empty. I need to get drinks to the table. At least this is something not affected by the ice issue. How are we doing on that, by the way?"

"Repairman is coming in this afternoon. Someone will probably need to make another run to the store after lunch. Even when it gets fixed, it will take that old machine a while to catch up."

With a wince, Rebecca hastened over to grab a few glasses from their storage tray and fill them. When the waitress stored the rest of the orange juice in the industrial-size refrigerator, Elizabeth turned back to the walk-in cooler.

"Beth, I'm not finding the health, nor the fire department inspections. Would they be filed elsewhere?"

Elizabeth pulled the handle of the cooler's door. It swung open with a satisfying *click*. She worked the handle a few times as Rebecca had done. Though it felt secure, it was a bit sloppy in its movement. She pushed it shut. Another *click*.

"Beth?"

Hmm. She'd keep an eye on it. After the ice maker failure, she didn't want to admit to Moses that something else might be broken. She shuffled over to the office door and leaned against the jamb. "I heard you. Nowhere here that I know of."

Moses slumped against the back of the chair and turned to face her. "Well, they're not in the desk files. Not the most recent, nor the previous ones."

"I think the previous owners had a home office too."

Stripping off the hairnet, Moses ran his fingers through his hair. "*Denki.* If that's the case, maybe the paperwork accidentally got packed up when they moved. I'll reach out and see if they've got it with them and if they'd send me the most recent copies. I'd really like to know what the last inspections discovered and when the next ones might be. In the meantime, I'll contact one of my daughters and have them take a photo of our last Ohio inspection and text it to me. The states might not have the same report, but they should be similar."

"I wish I could help." Her mouth lifted in a tentative, commiserating smile.

Her heart lifted just as tentatively when he returned it. "Right now, the biggest help would be if you could repair the ice machine. Without cost."

Elizabeth straightened from the jamb at the bang of the alley door and approaching brisk footfalls. "I don't know about the cost, but I think help has just arrived."

Moses lurched from his chair as a dark-haired Amish man, toolbox in his hand, paused to look about the kitchen.

"Hi. I'm Aaron Raber. I understand you need some ice."

"And lots of it." Moses shook the young man's hand in a hearty clasp. "Glad to see you. Especially this morning instead of this afternoon."

Aaron grinned. "I got done a little quicker on the last job than I anticipated. And I figured I'd better hurry, with the Dew Drop the best restaurant in town and me hoping to take my wife out to supper. With one not yet crawling and another one on the w—" His cheeks flushed. "Well… um… Miriam has been a little more tired lately." Now his grin was stretched from ear to ear.

Elizabeth suppressed her own smile at the man's excitement over his wife's pregnancy. After a quick glance at Moses, though, any inclination to smile faded. A child— many children, in fact—was something she'd hoped to share with this man. A precious something he'd shared with someone else.

"You get it fixed by that time and your beverages are on the house. In fact—" Moses clapped his hands together "—you get us ice by suppertime, and both your meals are on the house."

"I better get to work, then." After a quick scan of the kitchen, Aaron crossed to the ice machine, squatted in front of it and set his toolbox down. "She is a bit of an old girl, isn't she."

Elizabeth scowled. "Even us old girls have our uses."

Aaron squinted up at her. "You've got years and years left in you. I intend to make sure this thing does as well."

Moses patted the young man's shoulder. "I like the sound of that. We'll get out of your way, then, and let you get to it."

Elizabeth watched as Moses checked the ice bin on the soda dispenser before pivoting in the direction of the walk-in freezer. Limping to her stool at the counter, she sighed. She might have years left in her. But lately, she was starting to regret the ones that had already passed by.

Chapter Nine

"I don't know why we're sitting out here on the porch. Even though it's a Visiting Sunday, no one is going to show up."

Elizabeth flicked a glance at the dog, which, duck in mouth, was stretched out on its well-worn blanket.

"But it would be nice if someone would come over today." She sighed. "Considering." Considering it was her birthday. One she'd always, even when there might be no one else, spent together with her twin. But Emma had a family now. A husband and a granddaughter. While she had... Elizabeth's gaze slid again to her companion on the far side of the porch. Her shoulders rose and fell on another extended sigh. She had a dog who was still here after a week, even though she'd asked Moses daily since he'd left the creature when he was going to find other arrangements for it.

Under her attention, the dog thumped its tail against the boards. Cocking her head, Elizabeth studied the animal's gray muzzle and tolerant brown eyes. As far as dogs went, it wasn't a bad animal to have around. It minded its own business, staying away when she pointed at it while warily setting out food and fresh water. It was actually kind of... pleasant to have something to talk to while sitting on the porch on a surprisingly warm spring day, instead of alone, knowing the rest of the world had something better to do than visit her on her birthday.

Elizabeth grimaced. "I'm wallowing in self-pity. If I wade in any deeper, I'll be up to my hips. Huh. I don't like to wallow. Wallowing is weak. I may be alone, but that just means there's no one to control me. No one but me, and *Gott* of course, to determine my course in life. No one to disappoint, or be disappointed by. No one to take care of." Elizabeth swallowed against the sudden thickness in her throat. The last aspect wasn't making her feel any better.

The dog dropped its chin on its outstretched front legs. It echoed her earlier sigh.

"Except you, I guess. I'm taking care of you. But you're an example of what I'm talking about. Look what happened to you. People let you down. They left. They didn't come back when you were certain they would. It…well, it can hurt." Elizabeth crossed her arms over her chest. "If you let it."

The dog dropped its duck and pushed up from the blanket. Elizabeth's eyes widened and she tensed when it strolled closer, tail slowly wagging like a pendulum.

"That's close enough." The dog stopped a few feet away and settled back down. Elizabeth, in turn, settled back in her chair. "You'd think Emma would've invited me over today. Maybe she thought my ankle needed the rest." Lifting her foot, Elizabeth examined the joint. Though she still limped slightly and the ankle gave her a twinge and ache if she stood too long, the swelling was down considerably. It probably would've recovered even faster if she'd done as Moses had suggested from the first.

Her lips twitched. RICE. Moses had ensured she abided by rest, compression and elevation as much as possible while at work. Thankfully, the need for ice was over when the ice maker was broken, as there hadn't been any to spare. Aaron had hired Wally that afternoon to take him to Portage for a part, but he'd earned the complimentary meals for him and his wife as the first wave of ice had clattered into the bottom of the old machine late that afternoon.

They'd had another scare later in the week, prompting Aaron's return. The walk-in freezer had quit working. Fortunately, temperatures inside never got high enough to risk any stored food before it was discovered someone, possibly the city workers while repairing the big pothole along with others in the alley, had accidentally blocked the air intake on the condenser.

While the freezer had risen in temperature, so had Moses. He'd been dotted with sweat to the point Elizabeth thought he was going to be ill before they'd determined the simple fix. Otherwise, well, the week hadn't been as awful as she'd thought it would be while sitting in church last Sunday.

Except for Moses's seeming encouragement of Daniel's interest in Rebecca. And Rebecca's returned interest in Daniel. She'd have to talk with the girl. Warn her it was no good to hope for a relationship with a man who was leaving. Elizabeth had overheard Moses mention to Sadie that he had a ten-year-old son staying with one of his married daughters in Ohio. Though nothing had been said and Elizabeth hadn't asked, for sure and certain, once they established everything was fine with their new purchase—which it was—he and Daniel would go home to his family.

Something else had changed from last Sunday. The prospect of Moses's departure didn't bring as much joy as it had then.

Elizabeth jerked when the dog bounded to its feet and woofed. Following its gaze, she watched a buggy turn into the lane. Her heart rate lurched and she rose as she recognized Moses's rented gelding. Smoothing her skirt and any wisps of hair that'd escaped her *kapp*, she walked to the edge of the porch. When the dog joined her, she sidled closer to the railing.

"Guder Nummidaag," Moses called as he stepped down from the buggy.

"Good afternoon to you as well. What are you doing here?"

His gaze dropped to the dog. "I came to see how Onyx was doing."

"She's still here. No thanks to you." When Moses turned back toward the interior of the buggy, Elizabeth hissed in a breath. "Hold it right there. You're not bringing me another dog, are you?"

"It'd have to be a very small one to fit inside this." Moses turned around, a layered cake in his hand.

Elizabeth lifted both hands to press them over her mouth. The backs of her eyes burned. She was afraid to ask. Surely it wasn't for her? She'd made numerous cakes for others, had even made the ones to celebrate her and Emma's birthday. But no one had ever made a cake just for her. Her round-eyed gaze shifted to Moses's grin and back to the perfectly frosted cake he carried up the steps.

"Why would you look so surprised? Don't you recall that our businesses in Ohio started out with a bakery?"

"How did you know?"

"What kind you liked? I wasn't sure. But as there always seems to be something chocolate around the restaurant, I took a wild guess."

"Nee, how did you know it was my birthday?" Elizabeth couldn't seem to make herself move. Her eyes kept darting between Moses and the cake. Her hands remained pressed to her mouth. Her heart, well, her heart was opening itself up for trouble again.

"Oh, Beth. I'd never forget. Not even after another couple of decades."

For a moment, Elizabeth forgot about the cake. Everything she was hungry for, was longing for, was in his eyes.

The dog woofed again. She and Moses both blinked. They turned as one to see another buggy pull into the lane. When they glanced back at each other, Elizabeth shifted her hands to press them against the heat that was rising in her cheeks. Moses smiled, a surprisingly hesitant one for him.

"It looks like you'll have to share."

For just a moment, Elizabeth didn't want to. Not even with Emma, who waved from the buggy as it pulled up.

"You have a dog?" Emma might've waved, but Cilla was the first one to pile out. "When did you get a dog?"

"Well, it's not really my—"

"Careful there. You don't know her." Cilla was halfway up the steps before her grandfather got his door slid open far enough to call out a caution.

"I will in a minute. What's her name?" Cilla squatted on the top step and extended a hand to let the dog sniff it.

In the ensuing silence, Moses raised his eyebrow at Elizabeth.

"Onyx," she muttered. "And she's not my dog. I'm just keeping her until—" she glared at Moses "—other arrangements can be found."

Cilla cast a side look to her grandpa, who shook his head vehemently even before descending the buggy steps. "You've got a cat. In fact—" Thomas Reihl glanced at his wife "—we've got two cats. A man has to escape to his own shop to get any peace."

Emma patted his shoulder. "Then why, when the cats are missing, do I always find them in your refuge?"

"They sneak in. I don't know they're there until I find them sitting on my tools."

"Well, if I can't have you, Onyx—" Cilla stroked the black head "—I'm glad I can visit you here at Aunt Elizabeth's."

"She's not my dog..."

Emma shook her head. "Don't bother. It won't do any *gut*." She lifted the cake she was carrying, one obviously made by a young baker. "I guess we need to get in line."

Cilla looked up from Onyx long enough to notice Moses and what he held. "Aw, you already have a cake."

"One can never have enough cake," Elizabeth assured her. "Besides, you made a friendship hummingbird one, my favorite."

"Really?" Cilla stood and brushed off her hands. She and the dog wore equally wide grins.

"Really." Though the words were for Cilla, Elizabeth held Moses's gaze. At least, until he winked at her.

As Emma passed Elizabeth on her way across the porch, she leaned in and waggled her eyebrows. "Did we interrupt anything?"

"Of course not," Elizabeth retorted, belying the flush heating her cheeks.

"Too bad," Emma whispered and continued on to the door.

"Can Onyx come in too?" Cilla gave the dog a final pat. "*Nee!* She's not—"

"She's an outside dog," Moses inserted. He too leaned in as he passed Elizabeth to add, "For now."

Elizabeth scowled as the door to her house shut behind her quartet of visitors. *That'll teach me to be careful what I wish for.* She patted her cheek to dissipate the heat still residing there. *I was enjoying the peace before they arrived.* But, struggling to maintain her glower, she knew she was lying to herself. As the murmur of voices drifted from the kitchen, her heart swelled so that, for a moment, she worried the straight pins at the front of her dress wouldn't be able to contain her expanding chest.

She blinked at the *thump, thump, thump* sounding from the location of her hip. Looking down, she saw the dog was right beside her, its steadily wagging tail banging softly against the railing. Cautiously pulling her hands up until they looked like chicken wings against her shoulders, Elizabeth edged toward the door before pointing at Onyx from a safer distance.

"You're not my dog." With that final reminder, she ducked inside.

Emma already had the cakes on the table, along with china and silverware, as she comfortably bustled about the kitchen she'd shared until recently.

There was a stark contrast between the cakes displayed on the table. While both were frosted and layered, the resemblance ended there. One was very appealing. The other was...probably edible. Thomas eyed Moses's masterful creation before glancing at his granddaughter's. He sighed. "I'll have a slice of Cilla's cake."

Cilla clapped her hands together. "Wait! Do you have candles? We have to sing 'Happy Birthday.'"

"I don't think there're enough candles in the house. And before we'd light them, I'd feel better knowing if Moses is on a volunteer fire department." Thomas caught his wife's arm before she could elbow him. He slid his hand down her forearm to capture her fingers in a gentle clasp.

Elizabeth's gaze lingered on their connection all through the ubiquitous birthday song. Emma was so happy now. Even though she missed her company, Elizabeth was glad for her sister. If only... Her eyes lifted to find Moses watching her. While the rest of the repetitive song had been a mixture of voices and enthusiasm, the last word seemed to hang in the air for several moments. *You*...

"Too bad we didn't have any candles. Now you can't make a wish."

At Cilla's words, Elizabeth turned away to go to a drawer for a knife to cut the cake. *I already did. I just don't know if I'm brave enough to accept it being granted.* She handed the knife to Cilla, who hovered over the cakes.

The girl carefully touched a knife to the center of her lopsided cake. "Do you want a big piece, Grandpa?"

He smiled at the granddaughter who, until a year ago, he hadn't known existed. "The biggest." His eyes rounded as a quarter of the cake was plopped onto a plate and handed to him. Below his beard, his throat bobbed in a hard swallow. "*Denki.* For sure and certain, that'll fill me up."

"Speaking of filled." Placing her hand over Cilla's, Emma directed the knife to a location to slice off a much smaller piece before nodding at the girl. "I heard the wagon-wheel- and ankle-eating pothole in the alley was finally fixed."

"*Ja.*" Moses extended his plate for a slice of the humming-bird cake. His own flawless creation sat untouched. "When I contacted the city, they apologized. Said it was the first they'd heard of it."

Elizabeth's brows lowered. "But I'd told the owners. They said they'd contacted the city about it."

Moses shrugged. "Maybe left hand, right hand. Is the city usually pretty *gut* about taking care of such things?" He took a bite of cake and gave an exaggerated sigh. "Cilla, I might have to hire you to work in my restaurant. This is delicious."

The girl glowed with pleasure. "It'll have to wait until after eighth grade and I finish school." She slid a glance at her grandfather. "And Grandpa would have to give his permission."

Thomas took a sip of *kaffi* from the cup Emma had just set at his elbow. "When has my permission, or lack thereof, ever stopped you?"

"Hmm, it's been a while. But I'm trying to get better. And since you finally have Emma, I don't need to, well, work around you as much." Cilla's gaze lit as she shifted it between Elizabeth and Moses.

Her own eyes widening, Elizabeth hastily swallowed her bite of cake in order to head the girl off. "Mmm. This is *gut*, Cilla. Maybe I'll have to come over and take lessons."

"Aw. I think I still have a ways to go." Cilla studied the intact chocolate cake and licked a bit of cream cheese from the corner of her mouth. "I suppose it would only be polite to have a slice of your cake as well."

"I appreciate that," Moses agreed solemnly, though his eyes twinkled. "But I'm not sure my baking can measure up to yours."

"You made this?" Cilla cut herself a generous portion. "I didn't know men could bake. Amish men, that is. My grandpa can't. He's pretty useless in the kitchen. We're both really glad Emma is with us now. We're glad for more than her help in the kitchen, of course. But that's what made us really, really glad."

Moses rubbed a hand over his mouth as he glanced at Thomas. "I'm sure she's been a wonderful addition for a number of reasons. As far as me baking? Well, Amish men used to sew from way back. Did you know Jakob Ammann, the namesake for the Amish, was a tailor?

"Originally, the Amish in the United States were primarily involved in agriculture. In fact, several still are. But *Gott* has blessed many with large families, and with only so much land to go around within buggy distance of each other, we've had to find other ways to make a living in order to stay close. Sometimes in ways we wouldn't have thought of previously.

"Years ago, my family had a small bakery in the area. It ended up being too small for my folks, who wanted to ensure my sisters—I have several, all younger than me— could stay close. So when my *daed* heard a bigger bakery in Ohio was for sale in a market supported by the Amish as well as *Englisch* tourists, he bought it."

Moses paused for a moment. His eyes flickered and his mouth tightened. Elizabeth frowned at his reaction. She had her own unhappy memories of when his *daed* had uprooted the family and moved away.

He cleared his throat and continued. "It was our family's livelihood. Although I didn't originally bake, and maybe some other Amish men might frown on me taking up an activity they might see as women's work, I needed to do my part. Commercial kitchens can be tight places. Too small to just stand there and with too much needed to be done. So I pitched in. And learned to do something like this." He gestured toward the chocolate cake.

"My grandpa is good at a lot of other things. Just not food stuff." Cilla spoke around a mouthful of cake. "Is that where you met Aunt Elizabeth? In a restaurant?"

"Ja."

"Were you both working?"

Moses smiled. *"Nee.* I was a customer and she was waitressing."

Elizabeth rose and gathered empty plates from the table and carried them over to the sink. She remembered that summer day. Moses had come in with a number of other *youngies* who'd been doing the hot work of baling hay. When he'd flirted with her, much to the amusement of his friends, she'd dumped a glass of water on him, advising him that he needed to cool off, as the day's heat had apparently addled his mind.

"Your great-aunt seems to have a problem keeping control of drinks."

"Really?" If Cilla had been a dog, her ears would've been pricked up. Emma glanced from Elizabeth to the girl, nudged her husband and rose to her feet.

"Oof. That's a rather full stomach you're poking there."

"*Gut* to know. Then we'll just have church spread sandwiches for supper. Saves me from cooking on my birthday."

Elizabeth followed as they filed out to the porch. Before she descended the steps, Emma pulled her into a hug. "I didn't want to miss sharing our day together."

Tears blurred Elizabeth's eyes. Squeezing them shut for a moment, she returned the embrace. "I'm so glad you came."

"Now," Emma murmured, leaning back to give a significant look toward Moses as he came outside, "I'm sure you'll be glad to see us go."

Cilla stopped to pet Onyx. "Are you sure we can't take her?"

"Come on, Cilla." Her grandfather was already climbing into the buggy.

The girl gave Onyx a quick scratch between the ears before trotting down the steps and scrambling into the conveyance. "I'll see you next time."

Elizabeth waved from the porch as the buggy rumbled away.

"Kind of like trying to harness a whirlwind," Moses observed.

"*Ja.*" Her lips twitched. "Wouldn't have her any other way."

"Reminds me of my youngest son."

Elizabeth's faint smile froze. *He's not staying. He has a family to go back to. A family you don't share. He'll be leaving again. Soon.*

"Do you have any church spread for sandwiches? Daniel met some *youngies* from another district and they invited him to a singing tonight."

"I suppose I could spare a bit." Even though some of the glow from the afternoon had just faded, she didn't really want her birthday to end. It'd been too...*wunderbar.* They sat on the porch until the growing chill of the approaching evening sent Moses home. She hadn't even minded when the dog strolled over to lie down beside her chair, although Elizabeth kept her hands firmly in her lap. Just as she needed to keep her heart firmly behind its walls.

But this had been her best birthday ever. She watched his retreating buggy as the sun set behind it.

Dear Gott, *please don't let me fall in love with him again.*

Chapter Ten

Elizabeth wrinkled her nose as she raised the wooden side of the concession stand and locked the stabilizing bar that held it in place. Booking the little building hadn't been her idea. Moses expected them to serve *gut* food from here? For sure and certain, she was all for helping the volunteer fire department. She'd always participated in the Mud Sale, supplying cakes, cookies, whoopie pies and other treats for a booth that sold baked goods for the fundraiser. She'd bid on items to run up the price and even bought something every year, whether she needed it or not.

But other than the *Englisch* owners donating some paper goods for the bake sale, the Dew Drop had never been involved in the annual auction.

While wiping down the counter beneath the booth's wide window, she watched the growing crowd that streamed by. Along with the several participating Amish districts, local *Englisch*—as well as ones up from Madison and over from Milwaukee—came for the sale where quilts, furniture, crafts, farm equipment, construction materials and several other items, in addition to labor, were offered for auction.

Mud Sales, named for the mud churned up by the heavy foot traffic over soft spring ground, weren't at all new to the Amish. But having one in their area had only started a few years back to support an EMT service. That particular need taken care of, the funds received from the event now supported several different fire safety–related expenses.

Maybe it was time, past time, for the restaurant to get involved. Just as it was past time for Moses to leave. He'd been here three weeks. Surely long enough for him to see the restaurant was well settled. It was definitely enough time to ensure *she* was unsettled. Every day he stayed she had to restore her barricade. Renew her battle to keep from falling completely in love with him again. Loving meant being vulnerable. Elizabeth sighed. She was strong, but temptation was growing stronger.

She raised the other window opening of the small enclosure. At least when Moses left, he'd be taking his son with him. He'd sent Rebecca and Daniel over a few days earlier to clean the frame and plywood structure and prepare it to serve food out of for the day. Elizabeth slapped the stabilizing bar into place with a bang. It would've been much better to have sent over Rebecca and Wally. Or Daniel and Anna, the other waitress. Any combination but the two he'd sent together.

Rebecca and Daniel found time together far too often in the weeks since the Glick men had arrived. They didn't need additional opportunities to do so. Elizabeth didn't want either of them to get ideas. Not Daniel, thinking local girls were easily receptive to the charming good looks and manner he'd inherited from his father. Nor Rebecca, as falling for Daniel would only lead her to heartache.

Once the Glick men returned to where they'd come from and where they belonged, she could get everything back to the way it should be. *Including your heart?* Elizabeth scowled, as if the outward action would keep that contrary inner organ in line. With a damp rag, she scrubbed vigorously at a spot the two *youngies* had apparently been too distracted to notice, before turning to inspect her restaurant for the day.

Unlike Amish homes, the stand was wired for electricity. The bishop had huffed and scowled but grudgingly given approval for the power to be used for the event, since it was temporary and was being used to benefit the fire department, of which many Amish men were members. Roasters sat on the counter behind her, the aroma of barbecued beef, chicken and baked beans seeping from beneath their metal lids.

On another counter, homemade potato chips, cookies and whoopie pies were separated into small, individually sized plastic baggies. An old refrigerator, purring loudly behind her, contained bowls of potato salad. Moses had announced, *announced*—he hadn't even discussed it with her—the Dew Drop had reserved the concession stand for the Mud Sale. Once Elizabeth determined there was no talking him out of it, she'd suggested all sorts of things be added to the offering. Bags of homemade egg noodles, jars of pickled beets and corn relish, loaves of sourdough bread and pecan rolls, among other things. Moses had declined, wanting to keep the menu limited to prevent competing with other booths that might be selling those items.

Elizabeth had harrumphed, declaring if he insisted on doing something, he might as well do it right. But as she'd turned back to the griddle she was tending at the time, she'd smiled, pleased with his decision.

Rebecca came through the door carrying a large handwritten pasteboard menu. "Where do you want this?"

"Do we only have the one?"

"I think there's one for outside too."

Elizabeth glanced around the interior of the concession.

"Put it on the back wall. Hopefully everyone can see it there. Including us, to help calculate prices."

Rebecca nodded, affixing tape they'd brought along to the sign's corners. Stretching over the back counter, she lifted the floppy, uncooperative cardboard to the wall. Daniel stepped through the booth's door, his arms full of large plastic trays containing bags of buns. At the sight of Rebecca, he hastily squatted and dropped his load.

"Here, let me help you with that." His taller frame easily affixed the upper corners of the homemade sign to the wall, the tape covering evidence of previous menus secured in a similar manner.

"Denki," Rebecca murmured, her smile as warm as the barbecue in the nearby roasters.

Elizabeth rolled her eyes and bent to open the large cardboard box of cups at her feet. "The task doesn't require the both of you. While he's doing that, why don't you stir the beans. Or have all the serving utensils been brought in? Check to make sure they made it from the restaurant. Be a bit difficult scooping up the sandwich fixings, beans and potatoes with plastic tableware." When the only sound was the refrigerator's hum, she glanced over her shoulder to make sure her orders were being followed. The pair behind her stood side by side, eyes on each other and goofy grins pasted on their faces.

They both jumped and slunk a step apart when Elizabeth loudly cleared her throat. The two were becoming like a flower and a bee. Wherever the one was planted, the other would soon show up. And linger. But not on her watch. For unlike the bee and flower, there could be no benefit to these two hovering together.

Not that Rebecca was foolish, or couldn't hold her own. But the girl didn't have to. She could learn from Elizabeth's own experience. At her continued stare, the couple turned away from each other. Reluctantly. Once Rebecca went out the door, Daniel finished putting up the sign in a trice. "I'll just go get another load," he tossed over his shoulder as he hustled for the door. And Rebecca.

"*Wunderbar.* Now they'll just dawdle together outside. I'll give them a minute, then prod them along again." With pursed lips, she scanned the counters and shelves. They'd packed and brought so many things from the restaurant, the kitchen there was probably half-empty. Surely the utensils were somewhere in the two-wheel trailer pulled behind Moses's borrowed buggy.

And that was another thing. They'd closed the restaurant for the day. Closed it! Left a sign on the door advising they were at the Mud Sale and encouraging everyone to see them there. The sale grounds weren't far, just on the edge of town. But still, Elizabeth couldn't imagine how much business they were losing today.

Moses bumped his way through the door carrying another load of trays full of buns.

"You need to keep on top of those two. They flock together way too much."

He set the trays down, slid them under the back counter and added Daniel's abandoned ones to the stack. "That's what boys and girls do."

"There're other things to do. Particularly today. And other people to do them with."

She stooped to lift the five-gallon beverage cooler filled with fresh lemonade onto the counter. Moses nudged her out of the way and did it for her. Stepping back, Elizabeth quickly dimmed the initial rush of pleasure that had bloomed at his action. While accepting help might be fine for others, she was capable of taking care of herself. Something she needed to remember.

Moses watched as Elizabeth organized sleeves of cups into neat rows alongside the lemonade cooler and efficiently set up the rest of the service counter. Though Elizabeth may gripe about the couple, he couldn't fault his son's taste. Rebecca Mast was a *gut* girl. Daniel could do a lot worse for a partner.

So could he. He smiled as Elizabeth bustled about, adding containers of plasticware to the collection on the counter and ensuring everything, including the cash box, was arranged to her satisfaction. Elizabeth might not be every man's choice for a mate, but for him, she'd fixed his interest from the first moment he'd seen her.

He ran his fingers through his short beard. Was he finally making progress? She'd been…softening toward him since he'd brought out the cake. Correction, softening one moment and re-shoring her walls the next, kind of like taking butter from the stove to the back of the freezer. But he was making headway. He could feel it. *Gut* thing, as he needed to ascertain her feelings for him before he moved his unmarried children up to Wisconsin.

When Elizabeth turned to scowl at him, his grin expanded. With a quick pivot, he headed back out to the trailer to bring in another load. Catching Daniel's eye from where the young man was shifting through containers with Rebecca, Moses jerked his head toward the concession stand. With a sigh, his son filled his hands and followed him inside.

Before they were even fully set up, they were serving customers. The trickle became a steady flow as the day wore on. There was no time for Rebecca and Daniel to flirt. Any communication was used to provide service for the customers who continually lined up. The midday rush had slowed to a steady but breathable pace when Samuel Schrock grinned at him from across the counter.

"How's that horse working out for you?"

"*Wunderbar.* I couldn't have wished for a better one. Does your wife need her buggy back? Didn't mean to keep it for so long. The time has gone fast."

"*Nee.* She's fine. We have another one and I've been so busy at home, that's all we've needed. Glad to hear you're happy with the gelding. I hope to make someone else happy with my work, as later this afternoon they're auctioning off my offer to train a horse." After a quick glance at the menu, the blond man placed his order. His eyes twinkled as Moses set drinks and Styrofoam plates stacked with sandwiches, beans and potato salad in front of him. "I'll need some help with this." Looking over his shoulder, he called to a young girl who sat at a picnic table with an obviously expectant dark-haired woman and toddler some yards away. "Lily. Can you give me a hand?"

"*Ja, Daed!*" The girl bounded up and trotted over. Giving her father a smile to match his own, she grabbed the drinks and carefully walked them to the table before returning for a plate.

Samuel's eyes glowed with affection as he watched her. "She's my horse trainer-in-training. But if I'm not careful, she'll have us handling more horses than I can afford." He started to turn away with a plate in each hand before pausing. "My brother-in-law sure enjoyed the meals you provided him and Miriam for his work on the ice maker. Along with myself, there are others offering services for auction. Jonah Lapp is offering a day of carpentry. My father-in-law is offering to cover a day's worth of milking." Samuel grinned. "Of course, I think his sons will be the ones actually doing it whether they offered or not. I don't suppose you'd be interested in auctioning off a few meals at the restaurant? The Dew Drop is a popular place."

Moses rubbed a hand across the back of his neck. "*Ja.* Tell them I'll do two sets of two steak dinners with all the trimmings. I'll get you something for a receipt to hand out to the winners." Casting about for some type of paper on which to do so, Moses quickly jotted down a couple of notes and handed them to Samuel.

"*Denki.* I might bid on them myself. Aaron couldn't say enough about the meal. I guess that doesn't say much about Miriam's cooking." With a wink, Samuel was gone.

Moses sighed. He was glad to do the offering, although he already planned to donate all his profits from today to the cause. That, along with a lost day of sales, would put a definite dent in the current profit at the restaurant. Sweat beaded on his forehead and his stomach knotted at the reminder. Stepping to the back of the booth, he took a few deep breaths to resettle it.

It was the right thing to do. In a rural community, a volunteer fire department was vital. Many Amish didn't carry commercial insurance. The district leaders believed church members should be accountable to and responsible for each other. So they strongly discouraged anything that would undercut community aid and relationships. The better equipped and trained a fire department was and the faster it could reach and extinguish a fire, the better for the community.

When he returned to the counter, another face appeared across it that made him miss the horse trader's cheerful countenance. Bishop Weaver frowned at the roasters lining the back counter, their cords trailing like black tails underneath as they plugged in to the various outlets.

"You're stretching liberties. This is not the restaurant, where I was persuaded *Englisch* accommodations needed to be made."

Moses quietly sighed. His smile was courteous, but stiff. "I know. I only had a short time to determine and plan for this opportunity to serve the community. Which is why I'm very grateful you've given permission for us to utilize the shed's existing resources."

The bishop's lips flattened, but after a moment he gave a grudging nod. "Just don't think there'll be a habit of approving similar actions. Rules for the community exist for a reason."

"Understood." Moses handed the bishop his order. When the man turned away, Moses looked over to see Beth watching the exchange. He shrugged. Different districts had different rules and allowances. His bishop in Ohio wouldn't have blinked an eye at the day's use of electricity for the event. Of course, in Ohio, electric bicycles and solar panels providing power to Plain homes were also allowed and quite popular. He'd probably need Bishop Weaver's approval, or at least acknowledgment, for his ideas on updating and upgrading aspects of the restaurant when he could afford it. Moses grabbed a napkin from a nearby stack and blotted his forehead. He'd need to tread carefully with the community leader.

The afternoon passed quickly. With the auctioneers finally silent, folks settled up with their purchases and began streaming back to their autos and buggies. Elizabeth leaned against the counter. It had been a busy day, but a successful one. To her surprise, they'd served many more folks than they would've at the Dew Drop. Perhaps they'd even introduced some of the local folks to the restaurant who hadn't previously been customers. Maybe the concession stand hadn't been such a bad idea after all.

She and Rebecca were packing up the concession stand. Moses and Daniel had gone to harness her and Moses's horses and bring the buggies closer so they could be loaded to haul the day's remainders back to the restaurant. She looked over to see Rebecca, who—in between looking out the window to watch for Daniel's return—was scraping what little was left in the roasters into separate large baggies and labeling them with the date and item. Elizabeth nodded in approval. She might not've been the one in charge during a health inspector's visit, but she knew all foods that went into storage needed to be labeled and appropriately dated.

"Is it too late for some chips and maybe a whoopie pie or two?"

She looked over to see a dark-haired young man at the counter. On each hip he held a little girl, both under school age. The girls' eyes were round with hope. Elizabeth pulled a couple of baggies of homemade potato chips from the counter, along with two containing whoopie pies.

"You're just in time, Peter. They were my next thing to box up." She handed one of each to the little girls. The man frowned as he considered his daughters. Elizabeth recognized his struggle. He couldn't extract his wallet while supporting the girls. She reached across the counter and, with his approval, gathered the smaller one from him. The little one clung to her *daed* a moment before shifting both baggies to one hand and looping the other around Elizabeth's neck.

Elizabeth's knees almost buckled at the surge of emotion the warm bundle in her arms generated. It was like finding a missing piece of a puzzle. Like entering a home from a long, cold winter day to the aroma of fresh-baked bread.

But following the surge came a residue of regret as, from inches apart, she met the girl's solemn gaze. She would never have grandchildren. Not even like Emma now had with Cilla. Tension thrummed up her arms. She wanted to cuddle the girl—the rare opportunity—closer. With a hard swallow, she kept her arms loose.

"There you go." The man handed over some bills. Elizabeth shifted so the girl could take the money, then dipped the little one, now giggling, toward the cash box to deposit them. With a sigh, Elizabeth handed the girl back and was rewarded with a tentative grin once she'd regained the security of her father's hip. Elizabeth crossed her empty arms over her chest.

"Have a *gut* evening." Rebecca joined her at the counter as they watched the trio walk away. Both girls waved timidly from over their *daed*'s shoulders.

Rebecca sighed. "I feel sorry for Peter. I probably would've given them the food for free."

"I knew he wouldn't take charity. The man is embarrassed enough as it is, with his wife jumping the fence to the *Englisch*."

"Even if she comes back, she'd be shunned. He wouldn't be able to have anything to do with her."

"I don't know that he'd want her back. She ran off with an *Englisch* man. And even before she left, he was living in the *daadi haus* while she lived in the main house with the children."

"Still, so hard being a single father. And he can never remarry, as long as she's alive."

Elizabeth turned to face the younger woman. "They married young. He chose poorly. That's why it's very important to be careful who you take up with. And why you should put an end to this pursuit of Daniel Glick."

Rebecca's jaw dropped before she pursed her mouth until it was as tight as the opening of the nearby chip baggies under a twist tie.

"You know he's not going to stay. And you're not going to leave. Your relationship can only end in heartache. It's best to end it now."

The waitress slapped her arms across her chest as, jaw thrust forward, she mirrored Elizabeth's posture. "You don't know that. You don't know anything about how Daniel and I feel regarding each other."

"I know it won't work. I'm only trying to help. To protect you."

"I don't need your protection. While I gladly accept your direction at the restaurant, I don't need, nor want, romantic advice from you. You're not my mother. You'll never be my mother." Rebecca shook her head. "I respect what you've done. You've had to fend for yourself. *Ja*, you've done well. You have a *gut* job. But no real family. I don't want to spend my life like you. An old spin—" Rebecca jerked her arms from across her chest to clap her hands over her mouth. Color bloomed in her cheeks as if she'd been standing over a roaring fire.

Heat rose up Elizabeth's cheeks as well. She clamped her arms more tightly about herself. "An old spinster? Is that what you were going to say?"

"I'm so sorry. I didn't mean…" The whispered words were barely discernible from between Rebecca's fingers.

The backs of Elizabeth's eyes burned. Her mouth threatened to quiver. To hide the abhorrent weaknesses, she jerked around to grab bags of chips, crunching them under her tight grasp, as she stuffed them into a waiting box. The only thing worse than her hurt was the longtime waitress's pity. *Nee*, she wasn't Rebecca's *mamm*, but she'd worked with the girl so long, seen her grow up over the years, sometimes she'd forgotten.

To Elizabeth's relief, after a moment, Rebecca followed suit and began packing with alacrity. They worked in awkward silence in the small area, carefully giving each other space in passing. It seemed like an eternity before the men stepped into the shack.

"You two are certainly making *gut* progress." Moses nodded as he took in all the items stacked next to the door. Daniel looked first to Rebecca. At the sight of her trembling chin and red eyes, he shifted a narrowed gaze to Elizabeth.

"Should be all ready in a minute," Elizabeth tossed brusquely over her shoulder. "You all can load up the buggies and drive yours on to the restaurant to begin unloading. I'll stay here and finish cleaning."

Without a word, Rebecca filled her arms with containers and swept out the door. Daniel, his jaw locked, quickly followed suit.

"What happened, Beth?" Moses touched her arm.

Turning her face from him, she squeezed her eyes shut at the immediate and unexpected comfort of his contact. "Nothing. Nothing happened. It's just…been a long day."

"Something has upset you."

She shrugged away from him. "Please, please just do as I ask." Knowing her eyes were a little wild, she blinked rapidly and swallowed before meeting his compassionate gaze. "I insist. I want to have the building in *gut* shape for the next users. There's enough for you all to do loading and unloading the goods."

With a solemn nod and a last penetrating look, he turned to gather a load and carry it out the door. Elizabeth lowered the board on one side of the stand to block out the sight of the trio loading the cart. The sight of Rebecca's bowed head, of Daniel, draping his arm about her in attempt to comfort. The sight of Moses, looking with concern in the concession stand's direction as he loaded trays, now empty of the bags of buns, into the cart hitched behind the buggy.

Grimly, Elizabeth began wiping down the counter. This was what happened when you cared. You hurt. Other folks had called her a spinster, or "single sister," "undiscovered treasure" or "leftover blessing"—various nicknames of her single status over the years. It had stung briefly, kind of like a fly bite. But had been nothing like the gut-wrenching pain of Rebecca's rejection and unintentional jab. It was obvious the girl was upset by her words as well. Elizabeth sniffed. Hopefully it wouldn't affect their working relationship. *Gut* thing it was Saturday and the restaurant was closed tomorrow and it wasn't a church Sunday.

Had she been wrong? She was only trying to protect Rebecca. Elizabeth bit down to stop her lip from trembling. Well, she should've known better. It was better just to protect herself.

The three shuffled wordlessly in and out as they emptied the shed. Elizabeth cleaned it to the extent no fly speck or residual piece of tape from previous inhabitants remained. Finally, Rebecca and Daniel climbed into Moses's buggy and left.

Moses stood in the doorway. "I don't think you can get it any cleaner without dismantling it, Beth. Are you ready to go?"

"I suppose so." Lowering the final side, she secured it before following him out the door.

He locked it behind them. "I'll return the key on Monday. Not what you're used to, but it certainly did the job for us today."

Elizabeth didn't argue when Moses gathered up Scarlett's

reins. On the trip to the Dew Drop, she answered his varied conversational attempts with grunts and mumbled one-word responses. With a sigh, Moses stopped the mare in the alley behind the restaurant, set the brake and climbed down.

"We'll take care of this buggy. Once you get that one unloaded, put the gelding up and harness Rebecca's horse for her," he instructed Daniel before collecting a load from the back of Elizabeth's buggy and carrying it in.

Elizabeth sighed as she set her initial load down in the peace of her quiet kitchen. Letting the others carry things in—she wasn't going to admit her ankle was aching a bit after the day on her feet—she set to work putting things away. Under her watch, there would be no disruption on Monday morning by not having things back where they belonged. Through the propped-open back door, she heard the rattle of hooves as Rebecca's buggy left.

Moses entered, kicking the door shut behind him. "This should be it. Rebecca is dropping Daniel off at our apartment, though I imagine they'll go to the drive-in first." He set his load on the counter. "Are you going to tell me what happened, Beth?"

Ignoring him, Elizabeth opened the walk-in cooler door and carried bags of leftover barbecue inside. With a sigh, Moses picked up the remaining containers of potato salad and baked beans and followed her. He set the containers on a shelf, taking an automatic look, as Elizabeth had, to ensure everything in the area was stacked as it should be, with ready-to-eat foods always stacked above any raw meats.

"Well, if you won't talk about that, then you can tell me why you never order enough supplies."

With a gasp, she whirled from where she was meticulously, and unnecessarily, organizing a shelf. "I know there's enough. I always order enough."

He gazed pointedly at the cooler's interior. "Well, then. Maybe you're ordering too much. Excess inventory. Leading to more we have to waste out."

She propped her hands on her hips. "That might be a problem in your other restaurants, but not here. If it looks like there's an excess of something, we just run a special. A successful one. We dispose of very little."

"What percentage? A *gut* number is under four. And if you're that low, then why do you keep such a large dumpster? Surely it would be a cost savings to rent a smaller one or schedule fewer pickups."

Elizabeth sucked in a breath to retort when she noticed, above his grim mouth, Moses's eyes were twinkling. He'd intentionally distracted her. Knowing he'd get a rise from her. Knowing he'd jar her out of her troubled thoughts. She fought her own smile. He had. Though a part of her ached at her and Rebecca's discord, it was no longer a big cloud blotting everything else from her mind.

He'd done that for her. Knowing—though she'd never admit it—that she enjoyed their back-and-forth repartee. That she enjoyed his lighthearted teasing. No one, except occasionally Emma, had dared to tease her for years. Not since he'd done so decades ago.

It warmed her heart, even as the chill of the cooler's interior was seeping through the material of her skirt. Elizabeth's eyes widened and the chill was internalized at the creak of cold hinges as the door swung shut and a decisive, ominous *click* followed.

She rushed past Moses to grab the door's cool metal handle and tugged. Although the handle moved, the door didn't open.

Chapter Eleven

Elizabeth's heart lurched. Her stomach plummeted. Her palms began to sweat despite contact with the chilly handle as she jerked on it again. And again.

"We're locked in."

Moses frowned. The twinkle in his eye evaporated like a drop of water on a hot burner. "What? That's not something to joke about, Beth."

"I'm not." Panting, she jerked on the handle again. "We're locked in. What did you do? You were the last one through the door."

"I just followed you in. I didn't even touch the door."

Elizabeth wanted to argue, but he was right. Suddenly dizzy, she kept her hands on the handle. Lead congregated in her stomach at the knowledge she hadn't reported or investigated the issue Rebecca had experienced with the cooler door. Her head whipped up with a sharp inhalation. The girl had somehow gotten out herself. Surely they could as well. She yanked on the handle again. *No!*

This was all her fault for not addressing the problem when she'd known about it. She, who prided herself on her management skills. The guilt stung. So she did what she always did when she was scared or guilt-ridden. She stung back.

"Well, it's your restaurant. If you'd had it fixed, this wouldn't be a problem."

"If *I'd* had it fixed?" Moses strode over and motioned her back so he could test the handle himself. "I didn't even know it was an issue. I might as well add it to the growing list of other things that've been problems in this restaurant." He gave the handle a final, frustrated tug. They both leaned forward as they heard a few faint *pings* from the other side of the door.

"What was that?"

Moses's chest expanded on a deep breath. "I think it was screws falling onto the floor. Apparently, they've been loose for a while. I'm surprised someone hasn't been locked in before."

Elizabeth opened her mouth to respond. Only the explosive words didn't come. Dropping her chin, she pressed her hands to her cheeks.

"What?" Moses frowned at her silence.

"It has happened. Rebecca had trouble a few weeks back. She'd gotten herself out by the time I reached the door." Elizabeth's fingers, already feeling the chill, rolled into fists. Unlike then, there was no one to hear them. They were the only ones there and the Dew Drop was closed until Monday morning. Along with the surrounding stores that were also closed for the evening and weren't open on Sundays. No one would be around to hear, even if their shouts traveled outside the confines of the walk-in cooler and the kitchen beyond.

"Don't you carry a phone?" she blurted.

"I did, in Ohio. But I've been leaving it in the office here. I'm tiptoeing along Bishop Weaver's guidelines enough already. I figured if I didn't carry a phone, it would give me credence to do some other things. And since Daniel carries his cell and the restaurant has a landline, I was hoping that would be enough."

With a final pull on the handle, Moses turned from the door to survey the cooler's interior. He gestured to the shelves of goods. "At least we're not going to starve."

"How can you joke?" Elizabeth pressed her lips together to keep them from quivering.

Moses touched her trembling chin with a gentle finger. "Don't cry."

At his compassion, and his touch, a lump grew in her throat. The quivering increased.

"We don't have anything to dry your tears and they might freeze."

With a dispirited moan, she swatted him on the arm.

Moses rubbed at the abused area. "Ouch, it's cold enough in here to make that sting. Next time I'm locked in a cooler, I'll be more careful about who I choose for company." Turning back to the door, he squatted to examine the handle mechanism. "I don't think there's anything we can do from this side. Even if we had the tools."

"Will Daniel come back tonight?" Rebecca definitely wouldn't.

"It's doubtful. He's with Rebecca already and I'm assuming will be for some time, so he doesn't need the horse and buggy this evening and won't be back looking for it."

Elizabeth hitched in a breath at the reminder Scarlett and her buggy were still in the alley. The brake was on, so the mare wouldn't go far. Particularly since she and the gelding were friends and she had him for company. "Even when you don't show up?"

Moses slowly shook his head. "It's a small apartment. He sleeps on a pullout couch. If he gets home later, with the bedroom lights out, he'll probably assume I've already gone to bed. I don't suppose anyone will come looking for you when you don't show up at home?"

Elizabeth wagged her head dismally, her lips twisting at the sad revelation that no one, except now maybe a dog, would miss her. She hissed in a breath. No one would feed Onyx tonight. Nor Scarlett. Nausea flared at the knowledge both animals in her care would go uncared for. She lumbered over to where a plastic crate contained jugs of milk. Removing the jugs, she pulled the crate from the shelf, turned it over and set it on the cooler's floor. She tucked her skirt underneath her as a barrier to the chill and sagged onto it.

Propping her elbows on her knees, Elizabeth dropped her face in her hands. "I'm sorry," she whispered.

"For?"

She blew out a breath, her exhalation a brief, welcome rush of warm air against her fingers. "You're right. I should've told you about the incident. It happened on the same day as the ice machine breaking and I didn't want to bother you about it. It…would seem like too many things breaking down at once. Then, when it didn't happen again, I guess I just hoped it wasn't really an issue."

Moses pulled a couple of solid boxes from the shelves and stacked them on the floor. He settled onto them with a sigh. "Well, this would be a good time to have something propped against the condenser in the alley and raise the temperature, like happened before to the freezer. You doing all right?"

Nodding dully, she gave him a ragged smile.

"What I said before about choosing who I'd want to be in here with?" Moses tipped his head as he considered her. "I'd choose you, Beth."

This time she couldn't stop the tears. One escaped to trickle down the side of her nose. Turning her head, Elizabeth reached up to dash it away. When she was confident no more were following it, she looked back at him. "Why didn't you choose me before?"

"I did. You said no."

She was wrong. She didn't have herself under control. More tears erupted. Lifting her apron, she dabbed at them. "I wanted to go with you. But that would've left Emma alone to help our *daed*. I couldn't…I couldn't decide. So I…made you decide for me. I gave you a test. I did say no. Initially. I felt if you really loved me, you'd be persistent. You'd ask me again. And that time, I was going to say yes." She crossed her arms over her chest, against both the physical and emotional chill causing her to shiver. "But you never did."

Moses grimaced, his contorted face reflecting more dismay than it had upon discovering they were trapped in the cooler. "I wish I'd known."

She angled toward him until their knees bumped. Even that nominal contact warmed her through her dress. Through her heart. "Why didn't you ask again?"

He shook his head. "I figured I knew you. You're a pretty decisive woman. I figured your yes meant yes and your no, though it gutted me, meant no. So, licking my wounds, I went with my family to Ohio."

"And forgot about me," she added flatly.

"Oh, *nee*. Not at all. After I finished moping at your rejection, I'd determined if anyone could get through your stubbornness, it was me. I knew you were quite capable of ignoring a letter. I needed to be face-to-face with you, so I was planning a trip back to Miller's Creek."

Elizabeth's heart began pounding. Her fingers curled into her sides. "When was this? I never saw you."

"That's because I never came. My *daed* had a heart attack. For a while we didn't know if he'd make it. He survived, but he was very weak. Could hardly get out of bed, much less work at the bakery we'd just bought.

"So…" Moses scrubbed a hand over his face. "I did. My *mamm* and sisters needed a livelihood. We'd invested everything in the bakery. If we didn't make a go of it, they wouldn't even have a roof over their heads. They were depending on me. Besides, you'd set the example by staying in Wisconsin because your family needed you. I was going to prove my worth by working nonstop in Ohio because mine needed me. And after your rejection, I guess I needed to be needed at something I could succeed at. So I worked." He sighed. "And worked. I spent hours at the bakery. I didn't think it would be for that long. Only a few months for my *daed* to get back on his feet."

Elizabeth stared unseeing at the door that locked them in. *He was going to come back…*

"Then, after a number of different procedures to try to change the outcome, *Daed* died. We had an enormous amount of medical bills to pay off. The community would've helped. But as we were brand-new to it—had hardly been there three months—I couldn't let them. So I worked some more. I worked off my grief of knowing my father was never going to be a success at his dream. So I was a success at it for him." Moses ran his hands up and down his pant legs.

Elizabeth didn't know if it was because he was cold or, like her, unsettled at distant memories. Lost hopes. Past regrets.

He hadn't forgotten her.

"Some of my sisters had met and married local men. When the restaurant in town came up for sale, I saw it as an opportunity to expand the business and provide jobs for them. By the time I thought it was safe, that we were finally out of debt and my family was employed and secure, three years had passed. I thought about coming up, but I figured you'd long moved on. Had surely forgotten about me." He speared her with a look. "Because, while I hadn't sent any mail in that time, neither had anyone else."

Elizabeth flushed. She'd started numerous letters to him, only to burn them, some unfinished, a few having gotten as far as to be sealed in an envelope. But before she'd get them to the mailbox, she'd turn around in the lane. *If I never reach out, I can't be rejected.* After all, he'd failed her test...

Moses contemplated his hands as he slowly rubbed them together. "So when one of my sisters' friends—one who'd helped us out at the restaurant—always seemed to be around, I asked her to walk out with me." He smiled ruefully. "She was a nice girl. She was a *gut* wife and mother. We...made a *gut* team. And if I wasn't...completely happy, at least I was content. I think she was too. I think I did my part on that." His hands stilled into a steeple on which he rested his chin as he stared at the tiled floor. "I don't think she ever knew she wasn't my first choice. I hope not."

Elizabeth slid her hands down to fist into her apron. The back of her nose prickled. She sniffed. "I'm sure you made her happy."

Moses glanced over, his eyes remorseful. "I guess we'll never know."

Elizabeth swallowed. Did she really want to know about his wife? The woman who'd had him all these years, who'd shared experiences with him she never would, who'd borne his children? Children who might've been hers. She cleared her throat. "I know there's Daniel, and I've heard you mention a young son and some married daughters who were involved in your restaurants in Ohio. Do you have other children still at home?"

Moses straightened on his makeshift perch. "I'm beset

with women, both as siblings and children." The full-blown smile on his face belied his complaining. "I have two married daughters, and three teenage ones still at home, although I wouldn't be surprised if an announcement is made in church this fall regarding one of them. And bookend sons, with Daniel the oldest, and Jonathan, ten."

All that. And she had…a dog. Sort of. How different life could've been if she'd only trusted. Herself, and him.

She rubbed a hand over her forearm, grateful for the long sleeves of her dress. Even so, gooseflesh pricked underneath it. Surging to her feet, she strode to the door and tried the handle again.

"It's no use, Beth. We're going to be here for a while. Might as well make ourselves comfortable." He gestured to the racks that surrounded them. "Are you hungry?"

She shook her head.

He scooted her abandoned milk crate closer to him and patted it. "Might as well sit down, then. I'm sure your ankle is tired after spending all day on it."

Though she longed to join him, Elizabeth eyed the crate that nestled next to his perch dubiously. "Probably not a *gut* idea." Not for her, anyway. Too tempting.

"I don't know what you think I have in mind, but I'm just hoping to get within a few inches of the only other warm thing in here before we both look like Popsicles."

She reluctantly returned to sink down beside him. His seat was slightly higher than hers, as his stacked boxes were a little taller than her milk crate.

"I don't bite, Beth. If you do hear my teeth clicking, they're just chattering because of the cold."

She remained rigid. Her hands cupping her knees. Not only was being in the cooler her fault, but also the years she'd spent without him.

"Lean back against me, Beth. Would it fracture that stubborn spine of yours to do so?"

Not her spine, but maybe her heart. One that had already been broken once over him.

Ever so slowly, she relaxed her back and angled toward him. When she first made contact, she was as stiff as something left in the freezer next door, but as the heat from his chest warmed her, she couldn't prevent melting into him. Moses wrapped an arm around her shoulders. It was difficult to tell which was more tempting. The physical warmth now enveloping her shoulders and back, or the emotional warmth of leaning on someone for the first time in what seemed forever.

Though he wanted to shudder out an extended sigh at having her in his arms—well, arm—Moses carefully controlled his exhalation so as not to jostle the woman resting against him.

"We can get up and do laps later to keep warm. But for now, this is nice." When she shifted slightly, he kept up his mild patter, knowing it would help keep her, them both, calm. "When you hurt your ankle, we should've just bundled you, except for your ankle, up and put you in here. That way we'd know you'd at least kept it cool."

"You'd do anything to get me out of your way," she muttered half-heartedly.

The moments ticked by. Moses stifled a shiver as the evaporator fans continued to stir the air. What if no one came until Monday morning? No, he couldn't think that. Surely when Daniel got up tomorrow, his son would realize he was gone? *If he didn't think I've just left early on a Visiting Sunday.* Daniel could be a heavy and late sleeper.

Moses's arm tightened around Beth. Would they make it until Monday?

What if they didn't? What would that do to his family? Though Moses tried to steady it, to keep Beth from being disturbed, his breathing accelerated. They'd…they'd be all right. He wouldn't be leaving them with medical bills. The businesses were well established, though they would have to let the Dew Drop go. He wouldn't be putting his son through what he'd experienced. The knowledge did no good. His heart began to pound. In the chill of the cooler, sweat dotted his forehead. Pain shot through his chest. When he tensed, Beth shifted to see his face before he could stifle the spasm that crossed it.

She jerked upright. "What's the matter?"

Drawing in a ragged breath, Moses rubbed a hand over his chest. He tried for a reassuring smile but another abrupt grimace fractured it. "*Ach*, I get pains once in a while."

Elizabeth gasped and pressed a hand against her own chest. "How often? How bad?"

"Well, this one was apparently bad enough it chased you out of my arms. As for how often? They seem not to agree with Wisconsin." Despite his joking words, he frowned. "They seem to be coming more and more frequently."

Her eyes wide, Elizabeth looked more panicked than he was. She jolted to her feet and strode toward the door. "We need to get you to a doctor."

"Beth. We can't get out. It will go away. It always has." At least, he hoped it would. Right now, the weight of the restaurant's commercial refrigerator seemed to be on his chest and the weight of the world, on his back.

Elizabeth came back to stand before him. "But what if it doesn't? What if something drastic happens like it did with your…?"

He closed his eyes and concentrated on breathing past the vise that gripped his lungs. "Like it did with my father? That's..." He focused on inhalations. "My concern."

"What have the doctors said about it?"

Opening one eye, he regarded her through it. "I haven't seen them about it."

"What!"

Elizabeth's shriek echoed through the cooler. Moses winced. If anything would've alerted help, that screech would have. To his immense relief, the pain was finally dissipating under his massaging fingers. He scowled. She'd hound him until he told. And it wasn't like he could avoid her. "The truth is, if I were to see a doctor, then I'd know. And I don't want to know."

"And you call me stubborn? But there are things they could do! The *Englisch* hospitals do these types of things all the time. Even Bishop Weaver had heart issues a while back and they were able to fix him."

"*Ja*, they can. And they're very expensive. We don't carry health insurance like the *Englisch* do. I don't want everyone in the community, or my family, to have to suffer to pay it all back. I saw it happen with my father. I lived it." He winced again, not at the physical pain, but at the remembered weight of medical bills hanging over his family. The community had been willing to help, but as his father's oldest and only son, he'd absorbed the responsibility to cover the costs. "If something happens, it's *Gott*'s will. I'm not going to put my children through that for me."

"That's just..."

Moses raised his eyebrows. He'd seen Beth mad before, but he'd never seen her so mad she was at a loss for words.

She propped her hands on her hips so hard her apron bounced. "It's foolish. Prevention might help you avoid what your *daed* went through. I've thought you were many things, Moses Glick, but idiotic was not one of them. And now you've made me go and…and, well, you showed up again. And you're just…giving up! It just makes me want to…" With a huff, she strode again to the cooler door.

"Well, you've already screamed. It didn't help, so you might want to try something else."

Clenching her fists, she beat them on the door of the cooler. Moses shot a glance toward several cabbages shelved nearby, wondering if the sound's percussion was going to bounce the heads off their perch. When the echoes dissipated, Beth remained facing the door.

"Are you feeling warmer at least, with your outburst?"

Turning, she crossed her arms over her chest. "I don't feel any warmth in regard to you." But her furrowed brow, troubled eyes and the teeth worrying her bottom lip belied her tart words.

"Ah, Beth. You may not feel it, but I'm hoping you'll share it." He gave his chest a final pat. "I'm feeling better now. But after these things, I get chilled." He glanced around their confines. "Not that it would be any different than what I'd been feeling before the episode. But if you have any warmth at all to share…" His eyes met hers, all facetiousness gone from his expression. "I'd appreciate it."

Elizabeth held his gaze a moment before crossing the short distance between them. The milk crate screeched on the tile floor as she pulled it flush against his stacked boxes. Even the brief brushing of her arm against his as she plopped down brought Moses comfort. When she carefully leaned against him, accompanied with an exaggerated huff, he sighed. Lifting an arm, he wrapped it about her. A few moments later, he felt her own sigh as she sank against him, only to abruptly stiffen again.

"Am I hurting you?"

Ja, you are, Beth. But not in the way you think. I hurt for the years we didn't have together. For the experiences we didn't get to share. For the lonely woman you've become. For the impervious surface you project when I know you care deeply on the inside. Or at least I hope you do. Otherwise, what am I doing here?

Lightly, so that she wouldn't feel it, he kissed the side of her *kapp.* "*Nee,* I'm fine. Or at least as fine as I can be, given that by the time they find us, my ears might have frostbite."

"That's because you've lost your Wisconsin hardiness. And you've had your hair cut too short down in that Ohio community of yours." She relaxed fully against him, only to jerk upright again and turn to face him.

"Sell me the Dew Drop, Moses. I have almost enough saved. That would be one less thing you'd have to worry about. You could go home to your family. You could get some rest, more so than you're getting here, at least."

For a moment, he was tempted. For sure and certain, it would ease his financial concerns. But if he sold it, he'd lose his reason for being here. His opportunity to have another chance with her. And if he left again without her, there was no coming back.

"*Nee,* Beth. It's not for sale. You'll just have to learn to live with me."

She huffed. It was some time before she fully relaxed against him again. He gathered her close, drawing comfort physically and emotionally in the warm contact for a while, before rousing them both to parade within the small confines of the cooler for several laps and then settling back down. Over the next hours, they repeated the process. Over. And over. They'd even peeled labels from any available product and stuffed them inside their clothes for insulation against the long, cold night. Though there was no change in the cooler's light, nor that of the ones they'd left on in the kitchen, to advise the passing hours, Moses finally estimated it was nearing time they'd normally open the restaurant. *If* it was a business day. At least they'd made it through the night.

Beth was asleep in his arms. Moses smiled ruefully. He'd dreamed of having her there for years. Just in entirely different circumstances. He stared at the steel-framed door that locked them in. Where would they go from here? Would they have a chance for the future he'd always longed for? Beth was hard to predict. Maybe he should press for that conversation now, when there was no escaping for either of them until they talked it out. *Ach*, but with Beth, you couldn't pull, and you couldn't push. You just had to be patient.

He flexed his stiff fingers. His legs were numb with cold. Sighing, Moses rested his cheek against Beth's brow. It could wait. Either they'd have time later, or they wouldn't. For now, she was in his arms.

Chapter Twelve

"*D*aed?"

Moses stirred. Had he been dreaming, or had someone really called his name? Elizabeth shifted in his arms, the wadded labels they'd torn off and shoved into their clothing rustling between them.

"*Daed!*"

This time, there was no question.

"In here." It was more of a croak than a response. Moses cleared his throat and tried again. "We're in here." As he struggled to rise, Elizabeth lifted her head from where it rested on his shoulder.

"Praise *Gott*. I think we're being rescued." Moses attempted a smile as she peered at him woozily. "I'm not teasing, Beth. Daniel is here." After a few rapid blinks, she straightened away from him with the same stiff movements that were all his cold, reluctant muscles were capable of.

By the time he clumsily pushed to his feet, Daniel's shocked face was visible in the cooler door's small window. Moses lumbered over to it on feet that felt like blocks of ice. The metal handle quivered as his son tried it from the other side, but the door didn't open.

"There should be some screws on the floor nearby. Find a screwdriver and see what's possible." Moses winced when the condenser kicked on again. "In the meantime, kick the temperature up a bit." Following a quick nod, Daniel's face disappeared from view. But just knowing he was there... Moses's extended sigh exhaled a night's worth of worry.

Elizabeth came to stand beside him, arms wrapped about her chest, her brown eyes hopeful.

"He's working on it."

They could hear when Daniel set to work on the other side of the door. What felt like another hour from their end was probably only ten minutes before the handle wiggled again, this time ending with a definite, glorious *click*, as the door swung open.

Moses and Elizabeth stumbled out into the kitchen, the difference in temperature almost bringing tears to his eyes.

Daniel shut the door behind them. "What happened? How long have you been in there?"

"Too long. All night. Could you turn up the burners on the gas stove? I'd do it, but I'm afraid my stiff fingers would fumble with the knobs. And maybe get some *kaffi* started? I've been dreaming of wrapping my fingers around a hot cup for hours."

While Daniel hastened to do so, Moses went to the rack on the wall where his and Beth's outer garments—left when they'd arrived early yesterday morning and forgotten in the bustle of packing and loading for the Mud Sale—hung. He draped Beth's cloak about her unmoving form before slinging his coat over his shoulders. A moment later, he inhaled deeply as the aroma of freshly brewed coffee permeated the quiet kitchen. He guided Beth closer to the blue flames peeking between the metal grates of the gas stove.

"Scarlett?"

Daniel frowned. "She's still in the alley. I was more concerned about my missing *daed* when I saw her there. I'll go water and feed her now." His jaw flexed. "I'm assuming you'll need her to stay hitched so you can leave."

Holding her hands above the stovetop, Elizabeth nodded. Moses followed his son toward the door.

"I got worried when I woke up and you weren't there. And it didn't look like you'd ever come home. It's her fault, isn't it? Why you were locked in there?"

Moses looked back toward Beth, hoping she hadn't heard Daniel's harsh mutter. Under the black cloak, her shoulders were hunched, a stance easily explained by the cold. Still…

"It's nobody's fault. A mechanical issue that will now be fixed."

Daniel shook his head as he opened the door to the alley. "I don't know why you put up with her, *Daed.*" The door banged behind him.

Moses tucked his still-cold hands into his armpits as he considered the black-cloaked solitary figure in the midst of gleaming metal surfaces. *There's no "putting up" about it. For whatever faults she may have, Beth also has innumerous qualities. When you love someone, you love all of them. And I finally think she loves me in return.*

Scarlett needed no encouragement to head home at a fast clip. Good thing, since of the thoughts bolting about Elizabeth's mind, the journey home was not among them.

Daniel was right. Why did Moses put up with her? Last night's misadventure was all her fault. She, who prided herself on her competence, on taking care of others and herself, had almost gotten them killed. For a moment, when he'd complained of chest pains, she'd thought she was going to lose Moses. Realized she couldn't protect him from only an arm's length away. And it would've been her fault.

She dashed a hand under her nose but left the tears that

trickled down her cheeks unimpeded. No one was here to witness them. There was no one here she needed to be strong for, or to show that she was.

There was no more denying it. She loved him. And knew now that she always would. And she might…lose him. Again. Permanently this time. She couldn't bear it. *You'll have to learn to live with me*, he'd said. Though it had broken her heart, she'd learned to live without him. She would again. It was one thing to envision him living, presumably happy, in Ohio with his family. It was another to know he was just…gone. Like his father. And she would've been responsible.

Scarlett took the turn onto their county road, her ears flicking toward the buggy at the lack of direction. Elizabeth sniffed. She couldn't even take appropriate care of the animals in her charge. Scarlett seemed to have weathered the dereliction, but how was Onyx managing? Was the dog even still there? Her breath hitched at the possibility the animal might've wandered off. She was getting…used to having her around.

Just as she was getting used to having Moses around. That had to stop. She needed to make him leave. She'd thrown out the offer to buy the Dew Drop in desperation, after she'd thought she was going to lose him, though the thought of buying it hadn't crossed her mind since, well, since she'd realized how much she enjoyed working with him. Now, now she had to do whatever she could to send him home. Home, where she wouldn't know, or be responsible, if something happened to him. Home, safe in the midst of his family, where he had effective help to keep him from being stressed. Daniel was right. Moses shouldn't have to be putting up with things here.

Elizabeth straightened from her slump in the seat as

they approached her house, her eyes scanning the porch, searching for a figure that had become familiar there. When Scarlett swung into their lane, again without her aid, Onyx, her tail wagging, strolled to the top of the steps from behind the railings.

Elizabeth bursts into tears. Noisy ones. Scarlett jerked her head up at the sound. For the first time on the trip, Elizabeth tightened her fingers on the reins and guided the mare to the shed. After unhitching the horse, she brushed her down and added extra bedding to the stall, trying to make amends for her earlier neglect. The mare thoroughly cared for, Elizabeth trudged across the yard to the house and climbed the steps, drawing to a cautious halt when the dog blocked the entrance to the porch. Elizabeth swallowed, curling her hands into fists. She slowly exhaled when the cadence of the wagging tail increased. The old dog's eyes were not filled with the censure she deserved, but with welcome. With joy. Hesitantly, Elizabeth reached out and laid a hand between the old dog's floppy ears. She yanked it back when Onyx opened her mouth. And smiled.

Tears again filled Beth's eyes. "I've become a watering pot," she mumbled through a congested nose as she tentatively stroked the surprisingly soft fur. Beneath her fingers, Onyx gave a blissful sigh.

After what seemed like hours, days, Elizabeth's shoulders relaxed. Her animals had forgiven her. Hopefully Moses would as well, for what she was about to do. Onyx looked over when Elizabeth ceased her petting to press a hand against her stomach. He may not at first, but he would know in the long run, as she did, that it was the right thing for them both.

If Bishop Weaver was surprised to see her on a Visiting Sunday afternoon, his thin, bearded face didn't reveal it.

Elizabeth was just glad the farmyard was empty of buggies when she pulled in, that no one else from the district was there to witness her errand. Except for Ruby, his wife. Elizabeth generally got along with the bishop's wife, though they kept a wary eye on each other. As both were managing women, sometimes they butted heads.

This visit wasn't any of Ruby's business. Even though she was here, Elizabeth wanted to protect Moses; that was the whole purpose of this visit. She blew out a slow breath and followed the bishop out onto the porch, making sure the door was firmly shut behind her and the window to the kitchen wasn't open. Ezekiel Weaver sank onto a painted metal chair, glanced at another one nearby and looked at her expectantly.

Elizabeth couldn't sit. Bile was menacing the back of her throat. Clasping her hands together, she stared for a moment at the slouch-hipped Standardbred in the pen across the small farmyard. *What if he never forgives me? But he needs to go home. I need him to go home.*

"Well?" Bishop Weaver had never been the most patient of men, but consensus was he was better after his heart attack than he'd been before. It remained to be seen.

"I…" Elizabeth cleared her throat, her gaze fixed on the horse. "I came about the restaurant. I think you might've had a reason to be concerned about it." Her mouth was dry. Her fingers began to ache from where they were twined tightly together. "It's…possible he might be…doing things, planning things, that you might not…approve of." A drop of sweat trickled down her back.

"Moses Glick, you mean."

I can do this. "Ja." The horse in the pen swung its head around to bite at a fly on its shoulder. Elizabeth flinched as if she'd felt the bite herself. "He…um…he's using his cell phone to have his family in Ohio send up paperwork through it. I know some use of cell phones is approved, but I'd not heard something like that was." She drew in a deep breath. *Oh, Moses, I'm so sorry.* "He talks about replacing equipment in the restaurant. Upgrading, he calls it. He says not soon, but sometime down the road. And maybe expanding hours. I'm concerned he might do things not approved of in our *Ordnung*." All was true. Moses had talked of these things, but not in a definite way. Even so, at the time, her heart had lurched, not in rejection, but in excitement that he might be thinking of staying. Now she needed him to leave, for his sake and for hers.

"I see." Elizabeth finally turned to see the bishop scratch his chin. He sighed. "It is as I suspected. Moses Glick is a *gut* man, but things he's used to in Ohio are not all things that might work in our area. I suppose my mistake is allowing Amish from out of the area to buy the restaurant. But the *Englisch* couple had it for sale for so long I was concerned they would close it, which would disappoint the community."

"Let me buy it," Elizabeth blurted, taking a step toward him. "I will ensure it runs in conjunction with our laws."

"You?" The bishop looked at her as if she'd suggested she pull his buggy down the road.

Elizabeth drew back. "*Ja.* I have years of experience working there. I've been managing it since the *Englisch* left." She bit her lip. *Although, at times, not particularly well, it seems.*

"Owning a restaurant is not a place for an Amish woman."

Her chin lifted. "Other women in our community own businesses." Her sister, for one. There were others, but at the moment, none popped into her frantic mind.

"*Ja.* Small businesses. Not ones that are open so many

hours. Not ones that take so much time away from their homes."

But I have no one in my home. Elizabeth's face was frozen. She didn't have a family to take care of. Now, with Emma gone, outside of church and other community functions, her job was all she had. Not true. She'd had a dream of buying the Dew Drop. Though lately, that dream had been superseded by a dream from her past, a more tantalizing one. A dream of having a life with Moses.

Bishop Weaver shook his head. "*Nee*, I won't allow you to buy the restaurant, but I do thank you for sharing your concerns. I will address it." He pushed to his feet. "Was that all?"

Elizabeth nodded numbly and descended the steps. The short walk to Scarlett and her buggy seemed to take forever. Was that all? No, but it was more than enough. She untied Scarlett and climbed into the buggy, feeling older than she ever had in her life.

What have I done? I'm so sorry, Moses.

Chapter Thirteen

Moses darted another look to where Elizabeth was at the stove making gravy. Was she ill? She'd assured him before she'd left yesterday that she was fine. That she'd warmed up and had no lingering effects from their night in the cooler. But she'd been quiet this morning, which was unlike her.

She'd grown even more so when Rebecca arrived. The waitress had hesitantly approached her, but Elizabeth hadn't looked up from the sausage she was frying at the time. Rebecca had opened her mouth, like she wanted to speak, before her face clouded and she'd turned away. In Beth's defense, the girl had been standing at her shoulder, and with the sizzle of the sausage and general noise of the kitchen as they prepared to open, Beth might not've known she was there, but still, it was...odd Beth hadn't responded to her presence.

He frowned. What was between those two, anyway? And that was another thing—when had he been thinking of her defense? The *Biewel* said to give honor unto the wife as unto the weaker vessel, but he'd never thought of Beth as weaker. She wasn't normally a woman who needed defending. She did a *gut* job of taking care of herself. She'd be a *wunderbar* partner. Although she could be prickly if she didn't initially agree with something, she was a reasonable woman, with sound judgment, who eventually either came around to the way of thinking or explained—perhaps a bit vehemently—why she disagreed and usually presented a better idea. *Ja*, she'd be a *gut* partner for him. One he could trust.

And he'd find out what was bothering her after the breakfast rush.

The rush was just tapering off when Rebecca came through the swinging door from the dining room. "Bishop Weaver is here. He wants to talk with you." Her brows furrowed. "He generally looks unhappy, but this time, particularly so."

Beth's head snapped up at the announcement. Her eyes were rounded, her face pale despite the hot griddle she was working over. An uneasy feeling crept up the back of Moses's neck. He rubbed a hand over it. What could the bishop want now? Surely not another complaint about the power at the concession stand? Moses drew in a deep breath. Best not to keep the bishop waiting, but he'd rather spend another hour in the cooler than face the district leader.

He didn't have to go far to do so. Ezekiel was settled in the booth right outside the swinging door. Rebecca was right. The bishop didn't look happy. He looked like he'd downed a glass of lemonade, one made minus the sugar. Moses chose to stand, rather than slide into the booth across from the man.

Ezekiel didn't keep him in suspense about the purpose of the visit. "Moses, we're glad to have you back in the community, but I'm concerned you've brought with you ideas that do not fit with our district. And I'm thinking, maybe it's not *gut* after all to have an Amish man own a business such as this."

Moses folded his arms across his chest, above a stomach that had just plummeted. "I appreciate your concern, Bishop. I thought we'd had this discussion before. The concession stand was just for the day. Should we use it in the future, we'll make other power arrangements."

"*Ja.* You'd explained that, and it's not what I'm speaking of. I've heard you're using a cell phone not only for calls, but for sending reports from Ohio. Reports that could've come by mail. And that you have plans to upgrade equipment. Expand hours."

Moses stretched out a hand to brace himself on the table. His legs threatened to fail him. There was only one person who could've provided the bishop with this information. Only one person here who knew about the report he'd requested from his family, one person with whom he'd shared his aspirations for the restaurant, plans he'd thought she'd shared. One person whom he thought he could trust with his business. His life.

"When the time came, I would've run past you any plans to upgrade and expand." Moses's stomach soured. *When I could afford them. And right now, that time is so many years into the future, I might be talking to another bishop about it.* "As for the phone report, it was only that once. And after that, I've kept my cell phone in the office." *Something else someone knew, but apparently she wasn't looking for anything that would put me in a good light. Why would she do such a thing?*

The bishop looked only slightly mollified. "This is *not* your district in Ohio."

Something I know only too well. Moses pressed his lips together. Though he'd missed his family since he'd been here, had written letters, even used the restaurant phone to call his distant businesses, knowing he'd catch family there, for the first time since he'd arrived, he missed his

Ohio district. After decades in a progressive community, was he sure he could fit in a more conservative one? Certainly, he had *gut* memories of the Miller's Creek district, but maybe that was how they should stay. As memories.

As should the woman whose face appeared above the swinging door to the kitchen, a face that couldn't have looked any guiltier if he'd caught her writing out a confession.

"Was there anything else?" His gaze locked with Elizabeth, Moses wasn't sure if the words weren't both for her and the bishop. *What else are you going to get me in trouble with, Beth? You've wanted me to leave from the beginning. You were honest enough to admit it. Even pleaded to buy the restaurant from me. Although I didn't think you'd stoop to sabotage. And was it only this, or were you behind other issues we've had lately as well?* Moses had never felt more betrayed in his life.

"Excuse me? I'm looking for the manager on-site today? I'm with the health department."

He turned toward the neatly dressed young *Englisch* man who, smiling tentatively, had a clipboard in his hand. Blood drained from Moses's face. Though his face froze, his mind was rapidly going over all the checklists he'd been working on to ensure the Dew Drop was ready for this unannounced visit.

He cleared his throat. "I'm Moses Glick, the owner."

The man frowned as he referred to his clipboard. "I have another name down as owner."

Moses rubbed a hand across his mouth. "I purchased the Dew Drop a month or so ago."

The man's tentative smile was nowhere in sight. "Are you aware the health department needs to do a preopening inspection when a restaurant changes hands, outlining floor plans, standard operating procedures, menu, et cetera?"

Of the many things on Moses's mind when he'd bought the restaurant and arrived in Miller's Creek, that task hadn't been one. "But…nothing has changed. We have the same menu, same layout, same employees. Everything."

"I understand, but it's still required." In response to Moses's stricken face, the man sighed. "Well, I'm here now for a routine inspection. Let's see what we've got."

Moses didn't spare the bishop a backward glance as he ushered the inspector into the kitchen. Right now, he had other things to worry about than the church elder. As the swinging door squeaked behind him, they became the center of the staff's attention.

Moses cleared his throat. "Where do you want to start?" Over the next what seemed like interminable while, he followed at the inspector's elbow, trying to anticipate if the next stop on the checklist was up to standard. Tension was beginning to seep from his shoulders by the time they got to the cooler. Up to that point, the inspector had been nodding in apparent satisfaction with the staff, the kitchen's cleanliness and the processes that were followed.

The walk-in cooler door opened with a solid *snick*. It should've. Before he and Daniel left the restaurant yesterday, they'd worked on the door closure, testing it several times to ensure it worked properly. Still, Moses threw a look over his shoulder at his son to be on alert, just in case. It had been that kind of day.

"Why are all these labels missing?" The inspector frowned as he scanned the shelves. Several containers were stripped of their labels, the ones Moses and Elizabeth had used for insulation Saturday night. Moses knew what was in the containers and had intended to mark them accordingly when he had time. Intentions that were useless at the moment. He remained silent. Probably not a *gut* idea to mention he and another employee had been locked inside the cooler overnight recently. Moses sighed. The inspector made a note on his clipboard.

The man paused in front of the bags of leftover barbecue from the Mud Sale. He tipped a bag to read the handwritten markings on it. "This has the past Saturday's date on it. If so, it's expired and should be disposed of."

"That was the day it was made."

"Ready-to-eat potentially hazardous food needs to be marked with the seven-day disposition date from when it's opened or prepared." The man made another note on his clipboard.

Moses clenched his teeth. Elizabeth had been in charge of cleaning up the concession stand. She should've known this. His jaw flexed further at the memory of the bishop's early visit. If her intent was to sabotage, she was doing a *gut* job of it. He followed the inspector from the cooler on legs made leaden by seeds of doubt that continually sprouted as he thought back over issues the Dew Drop had experienced since his arrival.

The health department official turned to him, wearing a surprisingly sympathetic smile. "All in all, except for a few things that I think you can remedy in a short period of time, it looks good. However, I do have a bit of bad news." The man sighed. "I don't see a hand-washing sink within twenty feet of food preparation."

Moses's brows furrowed. "We have several sinks. There's one right there, and the bathroom is just right around the corner." He nodded toward the short hallway to the alley door.

The man shook his head. "That won't work. There can't be any impeding doorways. And that's a utility sink." He gestured to the one Moses had indicated. "You can't use a hand-washing sink as a dump station. No drinks, et cetera.

It has to have hot and cold running water to a mixed valve to a disposal station and be marked by a hand-washing sign. This is a priority violation. It will cease operations. I can ask for a voluntary closure. Otherwise, I can get an involuntary one in three days. I'd rather not have to do that."

Moses's mouth went dry. Bile churned in his stomach. For a moment, he was stunned, before his gaze darted around the kitchen, searching for a likely spot for the sink. But even when one was determined, it would take breaking through the floor and adding pipes into the walls of the old building. And money. Money he didn't have to spend.

"The restaurant has been open for years. Why hasn't this been mentioned before?"

The inspector shrugged. "I can't speak for the previous inspector. He left a few months back." He tapped his clipboard. "But these are the regulations."

Moses wanted to sit down. For a moment, he *needed* to sit down. He leaned against the counter instead. "Is there anything we can do in the meantime to stay open?" he rasped.

"Well…yes. You can set up a temporary hand-washing station."

Closing his eyes, Moses tried to envision what that might be through all the panicking thoughts currently bombarding him. He opened them to see the inspector eyeing him with mild concern. Moses blew out a series of steadying breaths. *Think! Think!*

He cleared his throat. "Would the one we used Saturday at the Mud Sale work?"

The man's expression cleared. "Yes. That would be workable as a temporary solution. You'd need water, soap and paper towels."

Moses turned to Daniel, who thankfully was standing within earshot. "Check on my desk. The file from the week-end is still there. Find out who we rented the station from and get one here, within the hour, if possible." With a nod, Daniel ducked into the little office.

"Sorry about the bad news. You have a nice operation. But for a few exceptions, everything else looks like it's under control. I have confidence when I come for a re-inspection, you'll have everything well in hand." The inspector glanced toward the hood over the stove-and-grill combo and winced. "I couldn't help noticing the stove hood. It's not under our purview, but I bump into the fire inspector from time to time." He shook his head. "I hate to tell you this on top of the other bad news, but I don't think this old hood will pass their inspection."

Moses was already so overwhelmed, the additional news barely registered. After numbly signing the inspection report, he thanked the man and escorted him from the kitchen. He wanted to stagger to the office and sink into the old desk chair, getting off legs that currently seemed insuffi-cient to support him. But Daniel stepped out of the office to report the temporary station would be delivered within the half hour from Portage and they needed to find a place to set it up.

Moses turned to see Beth's wide-eyed gaze. He returned it with a narrowed one of his own. How much had she known of this? Had she been setting him up for failure all along? Doing whatever was necessary to force his departure? His mouth drawn into a firm line, Moses jerked his gaze away. Even with the disaster of the impending expenses, Beth's betrayal was what cut the deepest.

Throughout the morning, Elizabeth—for the most part, at least enough to ensure she didn't put pepper in the pan-cakes or vinegar instead of oil in the waffles—kept her eyes on her work. But her ears, and her mind, which increased with tension at every timbre of strain in his voice, were on Moses. When, after the inspector left, Moses went into the office and, for the first time since he'd arrived, partially closed the door, she half turned in that direction before hesitating. What could she say when she'd caused part of his worries today? *I'm sorry?* She truly, truly was. She wished she'd never gone to the bishop. Her hand tightened over the spatula she held. She wished she—who could ably direct a group of women to prepare a wedding dinner to serve over four hundred and could manage a popular restaurant, or at least used to be able to—could direct her heart to making a decision. Instead of making Moses make one. Again.

Why had she no confidence regarding her heart, when she had an abundance—or used to—in everything else? Her lips twitched ruefully. Was she, like Cilla had suggested, a watermelon? With a strong rind to protect a softness that would never survive outside on its own?

She jumped at the soft touch on her elbow.

"You might want to make another. That one could be scorched on the bottom." Rebecca, her face apprehensive, nodded to the large pancake on the griddle, its surface cratered with large holes.

With a scowl, Elizabeth flipped it, shoved the indeed burnt pancake to the back of the griddle and with quick efficiency poured another puddle of batter from the pitcher nearby. She looked over as the young waitress opened her mouth. Before Rebecca could speak, Elizabeth shook her head.

"If you're going to apologize, there's no need. You were right. What you said was true. I...shouldn't have been trying to give you advice." As bubbles began to appear on the pancake, Elizabeth lifted the edge with her spatula to check underneath. She cleared her throat. "I was just trying to protect you from hurt."

Rebecca drew an extended inhalation through her nose to exhale it through her mouth, her tense shoulders slumping with the action. Obviously she was relieved to have peace renewed between them.

"I understand. And truly, I appreciate it. I appreciate everything you've done for me. I…care for you." Rebecca paused to worry her bottom lip as Elizabeth flipped the pancake. "But your life isn't my life, and your decisions aren't mine. I know it's only been a short time, but I think I lo…care deeply for Daniel. More than I ever have for anyone else. And you've seen me smitten with a few men over the years."

Despite her attempted joke, the girl's eyes glistened with tears. "I hope Daniel asks me to be with him. Though I don't know what I'll do if he did. I don't want to leave my home, with Jethro and Amos, and especially *Mamm* and the new *boppeli*. But I want to be with him." Rebecca lifted a corner of her apron to dab the moisture from her cheeks. She sniffed. "I need to get the tears dried off or customers will think I'm back here chopping onions."

"Or more likely, they'll think I'm berating you about something." The two women shared a small smile as Elizabeth plated the pancake and added a large dollop of butter to the edge. A festering sliver of tension eased from Elizabeth as she handed the plate to the waitress. She was glad harmony had been restored. Their workspace and community were too small without it and—the back of her nose prickled—she cared for Rebecca as well.

"You're a wise young woman. Seek *Gott*'s counsel and you'll make the right decision when the time comes." Elizabeth's gaze slanted to where Daniel had joined his father in the tiny office. A new shard worked its way into her as the door inched closed. In the weeks since he'd been here, along with teasing her, Moses had shared issues and ideas regarding the restaurant first with her. Lead pooled in her stomach at how much she'd lost that she hadn't even realized she'd had. Forcing a smile, she turned back to the waitress.

"And if he doesn't realize what a treasure you are, Daniel is even more foolish than I think he is."

Rebecca didn't defend her beau, just took the plate with a relieved smile and headed back toward the dining room. Elizabeth watched her go before dropping her gaze to the empty griddle. That was something she hadn't done as she should've, now and all those years ago. She hadn't sought *Gott*'s counsel. She'd trusted in her own. Elizabeth scraped cooked remnants of batter off to the side. *And look how that turned out for you.*

She was always better at giving advice than taking it. *Is it too late,* Gott?

The *Biewel* said to "Lean not on your own understanding." *Ach*, she'd leaned so much on her own understanding, if she wasn't careful she'd tip over. If she already hadn't.

Elizabeth tossed the burnt pancake into the trash as her gaze went to the closed office door. She needed to talk to Moses.

Chapter Fourteen

It was closing time before she had a chance. Moses had come out of the office, his face grim, to move straight into setting up for the arrival of the temporary hand-washing station. He'd shot a few looks her way while he'd done so. Looks that advised now wasn't a *gut* time to approach him, much as she wanted to.

Neither was it a *gut* time during the noon rush. Nor that afternoon while he was involved with the *Englisch* plumber who'd arrived to do measurements while they worked around him, preparing for the evening rush. After a brief discussion with the plumber in the office, Moses came out looking even less approachable than before.

Heaviness settled in her stomach like a foot-deep wet snow in a Wisconsin winter. In all the years she'd known him, Moses had never been unapproachable. Occasionally throughout the day, Elizabeth saw him touch his hand to his chest and felt her own heart jolt. She'd been tempted to forget his frowning countenance and tell him to leave to see a doctor, or at least go home or into the office and sit down for a while. But then she'd catch an occasional look in his eye, aimed at her, that clearly warned her to reconsider those inclinations.

One by one the other staff, usually with a wary parting look at Moses, left. The whole day and routines having been disrupted in one way or another, they were in an unusual hurry to get out the door. Daniel was the last to leave, though he, instead of glancing at Moses, sent Elizabeth a glare. Under its intensity, she dropped her gaze and concentrated on sweeping around the new portable wash station as the door banged shut behind him. When she finished the task, she put away the broom and, with a deep breath, approached the small office where Moses was working at the desk.

When he didn't look up as she hovered in the doorway, she tentatively cleared her throat. With a creak of the old chair, he turned toward her. At his expression, no more welcoming than it had been earlier in the day, her stomach tightened. *What am I going to say? That I was afraid of my feelings for him, so I looked for a way to protect myself? And the best way seemed for him to leave?* Would Moses even believe her? In her whole life, she'd never allowed an impression that she was afraid. And over something as simple as her…feelings for him.

Moses eyed at her expectantly. But not encouragingly. His flat gaze, knotted jaw and thinned mouth were far from the old Moses, whom she already missed. She pressed a hand against her stomach. *What have I done?*

"I…wanted to…" Apologize. For what? For doubting him years ago, or for doubting herself now? She swallowed. Best to start with apologizing for talking to Bishop Weaver. That was something concrete. And much as she wanted to defend her own actions, it had been ill-advised. Before she could open her mouth again, he spoke.

"To what, Elizabeth?" Instead of the heat she might've expected, would've even used herself in his situation, his tone was somber. Quiet. She'd have preferred he yell. *And called me Beth.*

Moses leaned back in the chair. "Are you going to sab-otage me some more? I think you've made your point and done enough already."

Elizabeth blanched at his words. Sabotage? She'd never do anything to hurt the Dew Drop. Or him. The prospect would never cross her mind. Except…it had. Or at least the thought of taking her—his—employees from him. Of starting a competing business. Of driving him out of one. Her shoulders wilted. Of stirring up an already unhappy bishop regarding some flimsy excuse about Moses's man-agement practices.

"You've been at the Dew Drop for years. Decades. Man-aged it for part of that time. Why didn't you let me know these issues existed before they almost cut my legs out from under me? If they haven't actually done so." The last was a mutter Elizabeth didn't know if she was meant to hear. Again, she couldn't deny what he'd said. The broken cooler door latch, the clean but worn machinery, the unfulfilled requirements from the health department. She'd been the one in charge recently. They'd been her responsibilities.

Now Moses's eyes, instead of flat, were sad, regretful. "You said it was a test, years ago, when you turned me down. Why did you feel you needed to test me, Elizabeth? When did I ever give you reason not to trust me?"

He hadn't. He'd never given her reason not to trust him. Ex-cept by having an interest in her that she didn't understand. It was herself she hadn't trusted. Her…desirability. She'd grown up knowing the value of being purposeful. Of being useful. Not of being desired for just…who she was, with nothing more demanded of her. How had he seen that in her when no one else seemed to? And with him, she'd wanted something more. Something she'd never dared hope for. How did one deal with such feelings? It made her vulnerable. Were his feelings real? What if he wasn't sincere and she'd let her feelings be known, only to look a fool? She could absorb being thought of as many things—humorless, no-nonsense, even bossy, though that stung. But she couldn't handle being considered a fool. She could envision the comments. *Isn't that funny? She thought he was really interested in her.*

When she didn't respond, Moses continued. "Now I don't trust you. And I have reason not to. You've resented my owning the Dew Drop from the moment I arrived. Can you deny it?"

Elizabeth mutely shook her head. That was true. *At the start. And then I fell in love with you again.* Though now, even if she admitted it, accepted it herself, he had no reason to believe her.

"Go home, Elizabeth." Moses sighed and ran a hand through his hair. For the first time since he'd returned, it was visible that the years he'd been gone had weighed heavily upon him. "I have work to do here."

She turned and trudged to the alley door. Even when her sprained ankle had been at its most painful, the journey had never seemed so long or so agonizing.

Elizabeth slapped the biscuits onto the parchment paper–lined baking tray. The inability to sleep over a guilt- and contrition-ridden night had prompted her particularly early arrival at the restaurant the next morning. Both feelings were strangers to her, except, it seemed, where Moses was concerned. Moses, who'd revived in her an abundance of emotions.

She needed to make reparation for what she'd done. It wouldn't be proper, or appreciated, to visit the bishop at three thirty in the morning, but as soon as the sun was up and she had a break, she'd go see Ezekiel and explain. Tell him...she'd been wrong. That everything Moses was doing with the restaurant was necessary, and if any Amish could own the business while still keeping true to their district's *Ordnung*, it would be Moses. Though the prospect of admitting she was wrong was bitter, like taking a dose of vinegar, it was the right thing to do.

In the meantime, she'd work even harder. She'd have everything ready that could be ready before anyone else came in. She'd show Moses she fully supported him in his decisions. Show him he'd have no reason to doubt her... Elizabeth dipped her cheek toward a hunched shoulder to wipe away the moisture that for some reason was trickling from her eyes.

Without turning, she set the filled baking sheet behind her on the griddle, lined two more with parchment paper and began transferring biscuits to them. She'd just work harder until he trusted her again. She sniffed. If he ever did.

That was another thing. Why hadn't the *Englisch* owners, with whom she thought she'd had a good relationship, communicated some of these issues? She'd overheard what the inspector had said. There were significant things that should've apparently been done over the last few years at least and hadn't been. Why hadn't the owners told her? Had they not trusted her either? After all her years of working there, of feeling proud—which she knew was a sin—because she'd been placed in charge, to discover she hadn't been valued enough to be apprised of these important issues regarding the Dew Drop? Well, it hurt. Elizabeth grimaced. Everything seemed to hurt today, except her ankle. Which was better, thanks to Moses's care. She sniffed again against the prickling at the backs of her eyes.

Those trays filled, Elizabeth grabbed the edges of the baking sheets, swung around and gasped.

Fire licked up from the stove. The edge of the parchment paper had slid off the pan to dip between the grates into one of the burners' short blue flames. The baking sheet with the parchment sprawled between the stovetop and the adjoining grill. The fire raced across the parchment on the sheet to crawl down the otherwise pristine grill's grease trough. When it reached the grease drawer, it burst into flames.

Elizabeth jumped back, dropping the trays in her hands. She froze, her heart pounding. In the split second before she jerked into action, the fire leaped higher. She grabbed a large measuring cup from where she'd been making biscuits, dashed toward the utility sink and spun the tap. Water still running, she dropped the cup into the sink with a crash. *No! Water is the last thing to put on a grease fire. I need to smother it.*

Frantically, she scanned the kitchen for a lid. *It's not in a pan. A lid won't fit over the grease drawer.* She pressed her hands to her head. *Think!* The fire wasn't taking time to think. It flared and jumped to pot holders she'd set out. Rushing to grab them away, Elizabeth stumbled over one of the baking sheets she'd dropped. She snagged it from the floor and tried to fit it over the fire to quell the blaze. Flames flashed out the sides. Heat seared through the metal. She dropped the pan and staggered back against the opposite counter.

Her hand brushed against something. She jerked it away before recognizing the container of baking soda she'd used in the biscuits. Snatching it, she flung its contents over the fire. It sputtered, but the blaze had grown too big. The oven mitts were fully engulfed. The flames lunged up toward the griddle's exhaust system. Smoke permeated the area. Elizabeth started to cough. Her eyes stung. Her face was flushed with the heat. *It's too much! I can't believe this!*

She turned from the flames, peering through the haze as she tried to recall where the kitchen's fire extinguisher was. She passed it every day. Several times a day. *Where is it!*

Her cough turned into a scream when she was grabbed and jerked backward down the short hallway toward the alley door.

Moses flung open the door and thrust Beth outside. She staggered into the alley and bent at the waist, coughing. He gave her a quick once-over, as much as the darkness in the alley allowed. No burns that he could see. Her coughs were slowing. She was breathing more easily. He exhaled in a gust. His heart, having clenched with fear when he'd opened the door to smoke and heat, finally began beating with some regularity. Jerking his shirttail from his trousers, he pulled it over his lower face and ducked back inside.

Why hasn't the suppression hood activated? Squinting against the smoke, he scanned the wall for the manual switch and slapped it on. He lurched back as wet chemicals sprayed from the nozzles under the hood's canopy. The hood's fans kicked in with a roar as they inhaled the smoke. But with its head start, though the fire staggered, the antiquated system wasn't enough to defeat it. Moses yanked the fire extinguisher from its perch on the wall.

His training in the volunteer fire department kicked in. PASS. Pull, aim, squeeze, sweep. Moses did so, spraying the remaining flames until no flicker remained. Following one last encompassing check, he stumbled to the office, retrieved his cell phone from the desk and staggered out into the alley to slump against the brick wall as he dialed 911.

Elizabeth was upright, and though her chest heaved in rapid succession, she wasn't coughing. Strands of her hair draped below her smudged *kapp*. Her face was white in the darkness as she gaped at him. She wobbled over to slide down the wall beside him. As he reported the fire, she buried her face in her hands.

Having finished the call, Moses slipped the phone into his pocket. He stared at the shed across the alley, where the gelding and Elizabeth's mare were nickering uncertainly. Both he and Elizabeth flinched when the fire siren began to wail nearby.

He looked down at Elizabeth. Had she set the fire intentionally? Determined to burn the whole building down in her efforts not to let him have it? He didn't think so. Didn't want to think so. Didn't want to believe she would do such a thing to him. To the restaurant. To the whole street of adjoined businesses if the fire got out of control. There might still be that danger, as he couldn't determine if it had already made a jump into the exhaust system that pulled grease from the griddle. Moses grimaced. The fire could still be working its way through the building.

Still, he wanted to reach out and touch Elizabeth's shaking shoulder. Offer some comfort. Make some connection that he was glad she was all right. But something kept his arms folded across his chest.

She'd been trying to extinguish it when he'd pulled her out, hadn't she? Then why didn't she use the fire extinguisher? Or manually turn on the hood like he had when it didn't automatically start?

It didn't matter. The whole building could've gone, and if he'd just saved her, it would've been enough.

His shoulders lifted in a chest-expanding sigh. He had a restaurant that was rapidly becoming an expensive burden rather than a benefit. Had the smoke reached the dining room? He hadn't been able to determine the destruction in the kitchen. Smoke damage for sure. Equipment? Probably so. If there still was a fire inside, there'd be water damage as well when they worked to put it out. Well, Bishop Weaver would be happy about one thing. In deference to some of the more conservative district guidelines, he had no insurance.

He dropped his hand to gently nudge Elizabeth's shoulder. "Come on. We should move away from the building. Across the alley, at least." Having helped her to her feet, he kept a hand under her elbow as he led her toward the shed. The old Elizabeth—a less guilty Elizabeth?—would've shaken him off. He retrieved a bucket used to water the horses, turned it over and set it down. Elizabeth sagged onto it.

"What happened?"

"I…I wasn't paying attention. I set a tray of biscuits on the stove just for a moment and the parchment slipped off to catch on fire on one of the burners."

"Hmm." The old Elizabeth was always paying attention. She wouldn't have let that happen. *But accidents do occur. I've had a few myself over the years.* At the sound of a siren and the sight of flashing lights, Moses looked up the alley, glad of the distraction from the conflict waging inside him.

A pickup truck, the decal on the door difficult to read in the still-dark morning, rocked to a halt beside them. Elizabeth pushed to her feet and greeted the man.

"Gabe. There was a kitchen fire. I couldn't get it stopped."

With an abrupt nod, the man looked to Moses, who added, "Between the suppression hood and an extinguisher, I think I got it. But I couldn't tell if it jumped into the exhaust vents."

The young man nodded again and glanced between them. "Anyone hurt? Smoke inhalation issues? Breathing all right?" At their nods, he continued. "Should be a truck right behind me."

He pulled ahead to the side of the alley, parked and rejoined them. Moses hadn't had much more of an opportunity to meet the man, who he learned was an EMT, before other fire trucks did indeed arrive. The two horses in the shed neighed nervously as large trucks, flashing lights and men filled the alley. Moses, though he was a member of his local Ohio volunteer fire department, stayed out of the way. As did a subdued Elizabeth. Faint light, visible between some of the buildings, was just breaking in the east when the firemen gave Moses clearance to enter the building.

"Should I put a sign out front that we're closed today, or do you think folks already know?" Moses attempted the joke as, with a leaden stomach, he viewed the disheartening interior of the Dew Drop's kitchen.

"Oh, don't worry. It's a small town. Word will get around." The fire chief gave him a sympathetic smile. "All in all, I know it doesn't look like it, but you were pretty fortunate. Good thing no one used water on the grease fire. I've seen that just destroy a kitchen. I think your equipment, once it's cleaned up, is all right, for the most part, though your suppression hood will need upgrading. Sorry we had to chop into the ceiling and a bit into the walls, but we wanted to ensure there wasn't any fire sneaking around in there. Do you have any questions?"

"*Nee.* I think I'll just look around a bit, if that's all right."

The man nodded and, placing a hand on Moses's shoulder, gave it a squeeze. "We'll get out of your way. Call if you have any questions."

Moses gave the man a smile, or what he could resurrect of one. "Thank you." When the fire chief left, Moses's dismal gaze drifted over the usually shiny surfaces that were now blackened and the gaping holes in his ceiling and wall.

Stepping over smashed biscuits littering the kitchen's floor, he pushed through the swinging door into the dining room.

The acrid smell of smoke hung in the air here, but except for a few holes in the wall adjacent to the kitchen, a few more across the ceiling and the accessory debris from those openings, the dining room had escaped relatively unscathed.

The room might have been unscathed, but his future wasn't. Moses sank into the nearest booth. The Dew Drop was going to drag down all his other businesses. He swiped a weary hand across his face and stared at the streaks of black that had come off it. Even if he could sell the restaurant— though it had been on the market for years before he'd bought it—he'd still have to put thousands of dollars into it first.

He'd failed. He'd failed all his family. There were even more folks depending on him now than there'd been years ago when he'd fought so hard to support them. And now he'd risked their livelihood for what had been a personal dream of his. A dream that had come apart on all accounts.

Moses's heart rate ratcheted up until it felt like it would bounce his suspenders off his shoulders. His face contorted at the bite of pain in his chest. He struggled to get his breath, each inhalation harder than the last. His head started swimming. His fingers came up empty as, grabbing for the table, he swayed in the booth.

Chapter Fifteen

❧

"Moses? Moses! Are you all right?" A firm hand gripped his shoulder.

Moses squinted to see Gabe, the EMT, at the side of the booth.

"Where do you hurt?"

"Chest." Moses reached up to tap it. It seemed so very far away.

The table screeched as Gabe shoved it against the opposing bench. "Breathing a struggle?" At Moses's nod, he continued in a calm voice. "Take nice slow, deep ones." The EMT drew in a few of his own. "Nothing too shallow. Don't want any hyperventilating on my watch. Ruins my reputation. Are you nauseous? Feeling faint? Is the pain radiating to your arm? Jaw? Shoulder blades?"

"Feeling a bit faint." Moses shook his head at the rest of the questions while Gabe checked his pulse and pulled a blood pressure cuff from the black bag he carried.

"Would you call the pain a squeeze or more of a stab?"

"More of a stab." He drew in an extended breath. "It's getting better."

Gabe paused momentarily in the process of strapping the cuff on Moses's arm. "Better?"

"*Ja.* It always does."

Gabe sat back on his heels, maintaining eye contact as he inflated the cuff. "You've had these symptoms before?"

"Ja." Moses tried another deep breath, closing his eyes in relief as unrestricted air filled his lungs. He opened his mouth to deny that he'd been having repeat issues, only to blink his eyes open in surprise to discover it was a relief to finally tell someone who could do something about it. "Several times."

"And they always got better? Do you feel all right in between the episodes? Not getting short of breath when you do physical activity like cleaning out a stall or climbing stairs?"

"Ja. They always get better. And *nee*, no shortness of breath otherwise. Only during the…the attacks." Moses cleared his throat. It was…uncomfortable calling what he'd been experiencing attacks. It made him feel incapable.

"I've got a portable EKG in the truck. You all right for a moment if I run out and get it? I'll be back in a flash. It'll show what might be going on with your heart with this episode."

At Moses's nod, Gabe disappeared, only to return a minute later carrying another black bag. Moses warily eyed the equipment the EMT removed from it. His jaw tightened as small electrodes were quickly and efficiently attached to different spots on his body.

Gabe consulted his readout. "Your heart is doing what it should. That's a good thing. But something is obviously up. When these episodes come on, is there anything in particular going on before the onset?"

Moses rubbed a hand over his now pain-free chest as he considered the holes in the dining room's ceiling and wall and the current state of the kitchen. Was there anything particular when the episodes overcame him? What had he been thinking of?

He frowned. They'd all related to one thing. This restaurant. In overextending his finances to buy the Dew Drop on a fragile hope of a youthful dream, he'd put his other operations, ones his family depended on, in jeopardy. A dream that was now shattered when the central figure in it had betrayed him. Obviously didn't want him. In fact, was the cause of this, the straw that would finally break his back.

"I've been thinking that maybe I've made some bad judgments." With his mind and his heart.

The EMT smiled. "I'd like to meet someone who hasn't done that once in a while. I'd also like you to go to the hospital." Moses tensed at Gabe's words, a reaction the man apparently noticed as he continued smoothly, "Though I can't make you, but please go to a doctor to confirm, as they can run some tests I can't do here. It seems like your heart is all right, but something is an issue. Are you under a bit of stress? Is there a possibility these might be related to anxiety?"

Anxiety. Stress. Moses furrowed his brow. He didn't know whether to be relieved or dismayed. He'd never thought about stress; he'd just dealt with it. The initial business when his *daed* got ill and died. The resulting avalanche of medical bills. Supporting the family. Expanding the business to support more family. The fear he was following in his father's footsteps. Concern his own medical issues would affect his family.

Did that all add up to stress that was physically impacting? To not sleeping well? He'd always faced potential failure by working harder. Until now, when this business endeavor hadn't been for the family, but for himself. And he was failing. Moses's shoulders sagged. He closed his eyes to block out the sight of the restaurant's damage. If only it would block out the knowledge of Beth's betrayal as well. He wasn't failing on what he'd hoped would be a lifelong relationship there. He'd obviously failed.

Opening his eyes, Moses sighed so deeply he thought every bit of breath, of hope, had left him. "No hospital, but I will go to the doctor."

Gabe met his gaze. "Soon? As in today?"

Moses nodded. At the creak of the swinging door to the kitchen, he looked over to see Elizabeth, her brown eyes as bleak as he'd ever seen them in her pale face, her fingertips white in their grip at the top of the doors.

He shook his head. "Go home, Elizabeth. You're not needed here. There's nothing for you to do. In fact, I think you've done enough already."

Elizabeth sank down onto her porch's top step and wrapped her arms about herself. Though her muscles clenched, it seemed impossible to clasp herself tightly enough. Was it a need for comfort? Or simply a grasp required to hold herself together? She'd always wanted—Elizabeth grimaced— *needed* some control over her life. Even if it was the smallest thing, like having her kitchen, or even her cupboard, neatly organized if the rest of life became chaotic. Which it seldom had.

But now nothing in her life was organized, much less under control.

Moses. Who'd sent her home today, saying she wasn't needed. With a hiccuping breath, Elizabeth closed her eyes. The Dew Drop. Even her mended relationship with Rebecca, since she'd just put the waitress out of work for who knew how long. Not only Rebecca, but her other workers as well. And how would the community respond when they discovered she'd set fire to a favorite business?

With all the issues lately, what if Moses didn't reopen it?

She, who took great satisfaction in her management skills, had sent everything tumbling down. Elizabeth bit into her bottom lip until it felt like her teeth would cut through the flesh. The *Biewel* warned, "Pride goeth before destruction and an haughty spirit before a fall." *Ach*, this was certainly destruction, and her spirit couldn't sink much lower.

The *Biewel* also said to "trust in the Lord with all thine heart and lean not unto thine own understanding." She did trust *Gott*. About many things. But what did the Almighty know about the restaurant business? Elizabeth snorted softly as her lips twitched. Well, He did know a good bit about feeding people. There was the miracle with loaves and fish. And one with water and wine. And manna. And Elisha telling the widow to fill up all the borrowed vessels from a nearly empty jar of oil.

Maybe the question was, after these past few days, what did *she* know about the restaurant business. If she didn't know that, which had been a *gut* share of her life, what did she know at all? What else did she have?

Elizabeth jolted and her eyes flew open when a cold nose bumped against her hand. Onyx stood at her side, her tail wagging gently, her brown eyes warm with empathy. With a sigh, the dog lay down beside her. Elizabeth didn't flinch away. Instead, she unfolded her arms to clasp her hands in her lap.

She echoed Onyx's sigh. "He believes I was capable of sabotaging the Dew Drop. To the point of setting it on fire. How could he think I'd do that? Not only to him, but to the restaurant's reputation? I worked for years to build that reputation. To do such a thing to my coworkers and customers? How could he even think I would?" She looked over at Onyx, who panted in agreement.

Elizabeth stared down at her clenched hands. "Probably because I gave him cause. Trust is a hard thing. Once lost, it's even more difficult to regain." She sighed again. "I don't even trust myself anymore. Everything I thought I was, I have cause to question. If I'm not capable, competent, what am I?" Reaching out, she laid a hand on Onyx's back, drawing surprising comfort from the warm fur.

Trust in the Lord with all thine heart and lean not unto thine own understanding.

The Dew Drop was closed. Damaged. As was her relationship with Moses. She potentially had no job. No purpose. What good was she?

Trust in the Lord with all thine heart and lean not unto thine own understanding.

Trust in the Lord. Elizabeth's brows furrowed. Her hand flexed in Onyx's soft fur. In the story of Elisha and the widow, how many of the woman's borrowed vessels had cracks or chips in them? Yet they still did the job. They'd still saved the woman's sons from slavery for her indebtedness. Elizabeth had made mistakes, she might be flawed, but...she was still capable.

She abruptly straightened.

She might not have loaves. She might not have fish. But she had a community. Would they work with her on this? They had on things before, but never on something so immediate or so important to her. She sucked in a breath. Folks might not like her, but they did respect her. Was it enough for this? Onyx scrambled up as Elizabeth lunged to her feet and strode to the door.

Before she slipped inside, she looked back at the dog. "I've got to go. I've got plans to make and people to see. But don't worry. I'll be back. You, and Moses, can depend on me."

Chapter Sixteen

Moses couldn't remember the last time he'd arrived at work after the sun was up. After yesterday's fire there hadn't seemed a reason to come in before sunrise. The Dew Drop wasn't going to be open today to early morning diners. It wasn't going to be open today at all. In fact, he wasn't sure when it would be open. In the dark hours that he'd stared at the unseen ceiling, he'd determined to repair and upgrade the restaurant to required standards. And sell it, knowing he'd be taking a loss. Still, even getting *some* cash back on hand reduced the threat to his other businesses.

Why didn't the thought make him feel better?

At least he could feel better after his trip to the doctor yesterday. His heart, when not impacted by stress, was fine. He'd apparently been having, as Gabe had suggested, anxiety attacks. While relieved he wasn't following in his father's footsteps, he was disturbed he'd allowed stress to get such a hold on him.

When the doctor heard his mutter, the physician had reassured him he was far from alone. Anxiety affected a good number of folks, many more than he'd suspect. It was the body's natural fight-or-flight response to perceived threats, many of which were no longer easy to fight or flee from. There was certainly no reason to be ashamed.

When the physician mentioned options of medication or visiting with another professional, Moses had declined, indicating he knew the root cause of his stress and would address it. The doctor had nodded, offered some breathing and other relaxation techniques and told him to make sure to call again if he had any further concerns.

Though Moses listened intently to the techniques, having now decided on a plan of action, he didn't expect to have any further problems. At least, not once the restaurant was sold. Would the techniques the doctor offered work on a broken heart? That was the issue that would linger.

It had been a quiet walk with Daniel to the restaurant from their rented apartment this morning. Reluctant to enter through the back and immediately face the damage from the fire, Moses lifted a key to unlock the front door he hadn't used since the day he'd arrived. He and Daniel had started the cleanup yesterday before he'd gone to the doctor. Later, he'd returned to spend time on the phone—the scent of smoke hovering in the otherwise undamaged office—searching for a replacement suppression hood. The existing one needed to be upgraded anyway and had proved it wasn't up to the job. The news he'd discovered in his search had prompted Moses to practice some of the doctor's relaxation techniques.

"What are they doing in there?"

At Daniel's bewildered question, Moses jerked his attention from the key he was inserting into the lock to peer at a trio of men inside his restaurant. Automatically twisting the key, he stepped back to better read a sign, one he'd just noticed, taped to the interior of the glass door.

"What does it mean, come support the restaurant at this temporary address? And where is that?" Daniel, reading along, obviously wasn't any more familiar with what was going on than he was.

"It's where the Mud Sale was held." Moses had made a sign inviting folks to the same address when the restaurant had been closed the day of the sale. He shoved open the door to the Dew Drop, Daniel a step behind him.

"*Guder mariye*, Moses."

"Good morning to you as well, Samuel." The horse trader was perched on a tall stepladder, fitting a precisely cut piece of drywall into one of the holes in the ceiling. "Always a pleasure to see you, though I'm a bit surprised at doing so here." Moses gestured to the two other men in the room. "Well, all of you, actually."

"These are my *breider*, Malachi and Gideon. It may not look like it, but as a *gut* part of Schrock Brothers Furniture— which I escaped a few years ago—they do know their way around tools."

Moses nodded at the two men, one bearded, indicating he was married, the other not. "Pleasure to meet you." He raised his eyebrows. "But why am I doing it here and now?"

"We have what you might call a vested interest. Malachi won the bid on one of the suppers you offered at the Mud Sale and is looking out for his investment. And Gideon—" Samuel smirked at the beardless young man "—is helpless in the kitchen and lacks any charm needed to coax women, single or otherwise, to cook for him. So we're happy to pitch in and get the Dew Drop back in business as soon as possible."

"Aaron, who I understand you met, wouldn't stop gabbing about how *wunderbar* our sister is." Gideon rolled his eyes. "So we chased him into the kitchen, where he's working with his *bruder* Ben." He tossed a roll of drywall tape up to Samuel, who caught it handily.

The bearded brother, Malachi, was on another ladder, mudding the seams of the wall's holes where the drywall had already been installed. He smiled. "Our vested interest is that you're a part of our community, and we take care of each other."

"Ja," Samuel added while he efficiently applied tape around the newly inserted drywall. "What's a town without its restaurant and what are we without each other?"

Moses had to swallow against emotions that threatened to clog his throat and make him sink from weakened knees onto a nearby tub of drywall joint compound. He knew the Amish took care of each other, but he'd only been in Miller's Creek a short month. Though he was familiar with many of his generation from when he'd grown up here, these men barely knew him.

"The compound will need to dry before it can be sanded and painted. But we'll keep an eye on it and get on those tasks as soon as possible." Malachi frowned sympathetically. "Still, it'll probably be the day after tomorrow before you'll want customers in here."

Though Moses smiled in return, he mentally shook his head. What point would it be to have customers in the dining room if there wasn't anything he could make in the kitchen to feed them? Safety regulations determined he couldn't use his gas stove or grill until a new hood was installed.

"I think the women have it taken care of until then. At least, that's what mine said before she took off in the buggy this morning, leaving me to wait for one of you to pick me up." Samuel scooted down the ladder to switch out drill and tape for a trowel and an aluminum hawk on which he piled drywall compound to its flat surface. He scampered back up the ladder, unimpeded by his awkward burdens.

"Is that what that's about?" Moses hooked a thumb toward the sign on the door.

"*Ja.* The Dew Drop has moved to the auction grounds for the next few days. Breakfast, dinner and supper." Gideon patted his stomach. "Makes me hungry just thinking about it."

Samuel slathered drywall compound over the tape he'd just installed. "Everything makes you hungry."

"Daniel, harness the gelding and head out there to see what's going on." His son didn't have to be asked twice. Moses wasn't surprised. Presumably, where the women were, Rebecca would be also.

"We got this covered here, if you want to go along. Otherwise, you might want to check on Aaron and Ben in the kitchen. It's been pretty quiet in there lately, and personally, I can't imagine brothers working together that well." From his perch, Samuel intentionally dribbled compound onto what he could reach of Gideon. Malachi shook his head from where he feathered out the plaster on the wall.

As Moses headed for the kitchen, he struggled to draw a breath past his constricted chest. For a moment, he blamed anxiety before realizing that what affected his chest and burned the backs of his eyes were gratitude and amazement. He stepped through the swinging door to find the facility much cleaner than he'd left it yesterday. The walls, already patched and mudded by the Schrocks, were scrubbed of soot and the stainless steel surfaces had regained much of their shine.

Aaron Raber and another bearded young man looked over at his entrance. Aaron smiled. "I think your equipment, for the most part, is going to be all right. And I heard about the need for the new sink." He jerked his head toward the other man. "Ben here is married to Rebecca's sister, so news travels fast. I know the *Englisch* plumber and I persuaded him to get the job done while you're down for a bit in the kitchen anyway. I hope you don't mind. Do you have a new suppression hood coming in?"

Moses shook his head. "I called on some." He winced. "But kept searching when I heard the lead times."

Aaron nodded. "I lived in Madison for a bit. Met some folks there. I might know a guy who knows a guy in the business. I'll see what I can do. Price?"

Moses drew in a deep breath. The price would hurt. "It needs to be done right. Let me know what you find out."

"Speaking of finding out, the fire inspector was by earlier today. Turns out the previous inspector was a *gut* friend of the *Englisch* owners. Knowing they were trying to sell and didn't want to put any more money into the restaurant, he let the hood pass."

The knowledge did little help now, other than make Moses feel like a fool for buying the restaurant sight unseen. He rubbed a hand across the back of his neck. But that was not the biggest thing he'd been a fool about regarding his return to Miller's Creek.

Where is Elizabeth? He'd made some decisions over the sleepless night. He'd realized that other than reporting him to the bishop, she hadn't been guilty of anything: the other issues had been unfortunate incidences, not deliberate sabotage. Though the efforts she did make to oust him cut bone-deep, he couldn't blame her. She hadn't invited him to return. She hadn't even known he was coming. She'd refused him once already. She'd built her life here and he'd disrupted it. If there was any fault regarding their reunion or lack thereof, it was on him. But just for a while, a precious while, he'd thought it would work out.

Moses grabbed some supplies and started working beside

Aaron and the man's quiet brother. "Seems like I've missed a lot of action already this morning. Which makes me wonder, how did you all get in today, anyway?"

Elizabeth turned from depositing money into the cash box when the women behind her called out greetings. Her tentative smile faded when faced with a narrow-eyed gaze from Daniel, who'd just entered the concession stand's back door. His chilly expression didn't deter Rebecca, who bounced over to him, a big smile on her face.

"Isn't it *wunderbar*?" She gestured to the substantial crowd eating at picnic tables outside and the busy activity inside. An array of devices was lined along the concession's interior counter. Amish women tended pancakes and scrambled eggs on griddles and sausages in electric skillets. Other women served fresh-made doughnuts, pecan and sweet rolls, or were filling urns with coffee from large electric pots to take outside and refill cups. The corresponding aromas wafted through the building.

"And we have more food coming for dinner and, later, for supper."

Daniel frowned. "Where did you get the electric equipment?"

"Our *Englisch* neighbors provided it. They were happy to help the Dew Drop."

"But how did it all get arranged so quickly? *Daed* and I had no idea what was going on this morning when we saw men working inside the restaurant and saw the sign on the door."

"*Ja!* Everyone came to help. We'll do it all again here tomorrow. Then the men estimate we might be able to move back into the kitchen after that."

Daniel shook his head. "We can't cook on the stove or griddle without a hood."

"*Ja*, but we'll fix things where that won't be needed."

"What can be fixed without a stove or griddle in a commercial restaurant?" Daniel crossed his arms over his chest. Elizabeth raised an eyebrow when Rebecca swatted him on the shoulder.

"It'll be a temporary menu, but there're plenty of things to be served. Specialty hot dogs, baked chicken, salads, cold sandwiches, soups, caramel popcorn. You've worked in restaurants for years, or so you've told me. Use your imagination. And look." Rebecca gestured to the continual flow of customers. "Folks are excited to do whatever they can to support the restaurant."

"Did you come up with this?" Daniel uncrossed his arms to grab one of Rebecca's hands. His smile at the waitress made Elizabeth press a hand against her stomach and turn away in envy and regret. Once upon a time, Moses had looked at her that way. She hadn't trusted it or him. She hadn't trusted how he'd made her feel. Now it was too late.

"Some of them are my ideas. The smaller ones. Elizabeth was the one who came up with the idea and organized everything. All the food and equipment and the workers here and the men fixing the restaurant." One of the other women working along the back counter called to the waitress. Rebecca grinned at Daniel. "I've got to go, but I'm glad you're here." With obvious reluctance, she dropped his hand to hurry over to the one who'd beckoned her.

Elizabeth had looked back when her name was mentioned. Once again, her gaze locked with Daniel's. He broke the stare-down to glance toward the door and back at her. Elizabeth drew in a long breath. As much as she'd once dreamed had things been different, this young man could've been her son, she knew reality was Daniel had been far ahead of Moses in not trusting her.

With a murmur to a fellow worker at the counter tending to customers, Elizabeth stepped outside. The back of the concession stand, with its lack of windows, was relatively private. Her shoulders tightened at the click of the door as it shut behind Daniel.

"You've got a lot of electrical equipment in there. I thought that was a problem for the bishop."

Elizabeth turned to face him. "Bishop Weaver approved its use for this purpose."

"*Ja.* I hear you're really *gut* at running to him."

Elizabeth winced. She was surprised, and a little hurt, that Moses had disclosed to his son what she'd done.

"*Nee. Daed* didn't tell me. I heard what the bishop said to him, though, the other day at the restaurant. And since that information hadn't come from me, there was only one other person who my father would've shared those things with."

Elizabeth's mouth tightened. She'd destroyed that sharing, that trust. Would what she'd arranged help make amends? Only *Gott* knew. But she'd had to do it, both for her sake and for Moses. Obviously, it hadn't made much of an impression on this young man who looked so much like his *daed*. Did it need to? *Nee*, she hadn't done it for him.

Elizabeth crossed her arms over her chest. "You don't like me."

Daniel mirrored her position. "I just wonder why my father did."

Elizabeth's stomach twisted at the phrasing. *Did.* As in the past. Well, the truth could hurt. "So did I. That's why I turned him down when he asked me to marry him years ago before he left."

Daniel's brows lifted and his jaw sagged slightly. "I'd

heard you two had a past, but…*Daed* asked you to marry him?"

"*Ja.* You could've been my son. Frightening, isn't it?"

Daniel's mouth twitched toward a smile. "I think I'd rather be stuck in the cooler for a week than have suffered that fate."

"Then I guess you can thank me."

Daniel unfolded his arms to rub a hand across the back of his neck, a gesture so like his father's that Elizabeth hissed in a breath. "It seems I need to. For this." He gestured to the concession stand beside them. "And for arranging the repair of the restaurant. It's a big help for my father."

"That's why I did it. That's why all of us have."

Daniel shook his head. "*Nee*, that might be why you did it. But that's not why a whole community dropped what they were doing to give you all the time you need."

Elizabeth frowned. "They're not giving it to me. They're giving it to Moses. To the Dew Drop."

"They don't know us. For sure and certain, they'd always be willing to help another in need. But right now, they're doing it for you because you asked them to. Just as Rebecca would do anything for you, should you only say the word. She likes you." Again there was a flicker of a smile on the young man's face. "I don't know why."

Elizabeth pressed a hand to her mouth. Respect from others, she'd always wanted, almost expected. But affection? It was more than she'd ever hoped for. Blinking back rebellious tears, she muttered, "You better not hurt her."

Daniel grimaced. "I don't intend to. I plan to ask to marry her. Hopefully she's wiser than you and will say *ja* to a Glick man."

The advice was years, decades, too late. "It will be hard on her to move."

Another grimace. "I know. It's a problem. With the fire, and other issues, I don't know what *Daed*'s plans are for the Dew Drop. I know he's worried about finances. If I have to, though, in order to stay, I'll find something else to do here. I don't want Rebecca to have to leave her family and community."

Elizabeth tapped her fingers softly against her mouth to hide her temptation to smile. It wouldn't do to reveal to the young man that she was softening toward him. "You're not so bad after all."

Daniel narrowed his eyes at her. "I could say the same. But I won't." Though before he glanced away, his smile did. "Now, what can I do to help?"

Elizabeth held her breath as she entered the restaurant's alley door. Was Moses still here? As Daniel was at the concession stand helping Rebecca clean up for the evening, she couldn't tell by the absence of the gelding in the little shed. There were no other horses or buggies around, so the other men were finished working for the day. No surprise, as it was after seven o'clock. They'd surely gone home to chores and suppers made of leftover food from the day that she'd insisted her Amish helpers take home.

After her conversation with Daniel, she'd gone back into the stand with a new awareness. When the other women had smiled at her as they'd dodged each other working in the small space, she'd tentatively smiled back. And hesitantly returned the waves, when they'd left, tired but satisfied by the day, to prepare to do it all again tomorrow.

Her stride faltered when she heard the sound of water and a *clang* ahead, indicating someone was indeed still in the kitchen. Who would it be but Moses? Drawing in a long breath, one wonderfully devoid of any scent of smoke, she stepped around the corner.

She paused, amazed at the change in the kitchen from when she'd last seen it. The stainless steel surfaces gleamed again. Patches on the wall stood out like Band-Aids on a tanned arm, but holes no longer gaped throughout the kitchen. A new sink with hot and cold faucets had been installed along a wall.

Moses was at the dishwashing station, washing all the pots, pans and dishes that had been exposed to the smoke and residue from the fire. His back to her, he wasn't aware of her arrival. Quietly setting the items she'd brought from the concession stand on a counter, Elizabeth crossed to where he was working and began putting away the dried containers.

He turned at the quiet clatter as she stacked two of them together. A tired smile crossed his face. "Beth."

Hope flashed through her at the name. Had she been forgiven? Could they…start again? And this time, succeed despite previous failures?

"I hear I need to thank you. For this—" Moses gestured toward the kitchen. "And for what I heard were *wunderbar* meals at the concession stand."

"It was the least I could do after…well, after." While Moses's thanks were appreciated, what she was looking for was his forgiveness. Was it possible? To receive one, would she need to apologize? Would that make her seem weak? Her heart racing, Elizabeth grabbed another couple of pots and stowed them. "I see the new sink is installed. That should make the health inspector happy."

"*Ja.* And a hood is on order, with a much shorter lead time than I could've hoped. The fire department is giving back my donation from the Mud Sale. They told me to put it toward the purchase of the hood, as it is fire-related and needed by the restaurant, which is needed by the town. I tried to turn them down, but they insisted." Moses shook his head, his eyes revealing how moved he was by the gesture.

He was sharing plans about the restaurant with her again. It was a *gut* sign, wasn't it? They could overcome the obstacles she'd created. They could work together. The prospect filled Elizabeth with something she didn't immediately recognize. Was this…joy? What a wonderful sensation! She'd only felt this anticipation, this pleasure, when working with Moses. Maybe, after he realized how well they could collaborate, he would propose again. And this time, this time, she would say yes.

Moses shut off the water and turned toward her with a rueful smile. "I have a question for you."

Afraid she'd drop the pan in her hand, Elizabeth carefully set it down on the counter. Maybe she didn't have to wait. Was he already asking? Her hands were shaking. She hid them in the folds of her skirt.

"You said you wanted to buy the restaurant. I'll sell it to you. Would you be able to have the money and wrap up the paperwork on it before I return to Ohio?"

Chapter Seventeen

The counter bit into Elizabeth's hip as she sagged against it. Her heart was pounding in her ears.

Moses was leaving.

She knotted her fingers together and pressed them to a stomach weighted with despair. Several seconds ticked by before her mind, buzzing like a disturbed beehive, processed what he'd said prior to the words "return to Ohio." Buy the restaurant? For a moment, the bees hovered quietly. Elizabeth gasped at the thought of a lifelong dream coming true. And exhaled in a gust, knowing it came at the price of an even more important one.

She cleared her throat. "Bishop Weaver won't let me own it." Though far from thankful for the bishop's decree before, Elizabeth now held on to it like a lifeline. Anything to keep Moses here.

He rubbed his fingers through his beard. "*Ja.* Ezekiel came by to see how things were going. I think the possibility of not having a restaurant in town at all put a fright in him. We talked. I told him if anyone could run the Dew Drop well and aligned with the district's rules, it was you. He was reluctant at first, but he finally agreed."

Elizabeth deflated like an underbaked cake. "The price…" If the cost was him leaving, it was already too high.

Moses sighed. "I'll sell at whatever price you can manage. I'm sure you'll treat me fairly."

Oh, but I haven't. I've never trusted you like I should've. I was too afraid of being hurt. And now I've hurt you deeply. Which brings me the greatest pain of all.

Though the bees in her head had resumed their frantic buzzing, Elizabeth had so often nurtured and calculated the amount she had saved that she knew the sum to the penny. Her mouth dry, she named it. Her fingers tightened until her knuckles were white, hoping he'd refuse.

Moses blinked, and Elizabeth held her breath, knowing the price was too low. Her stomach dropped to the vicinity of her knees when he nodded.

"I'll ensure the hood, if not in place, will be taken care of. And will arrange to have everything else up to code. I have to admit, the money from the sale will be helpful in covering those expenses." Moses smiled sadly. "This…isn't what I'd hoped for when I bought the restaurant."

He lifted his hand. At his expression, Elizabeth freed one of her own, hoping he'd reach for it. Instead, after a brief hesitation, he raised it to rub the back of his neck.

"I'd hoped… *Ach*, never mind. Maybe it's for the best. Maybe my plans *are* a little too progressive for here. Besides, I miss my family. I'd anticipated having a reason to move them up, at least the unmarried ones." He frowned. "But so many of my siblings and children are woven into their communities in Ohio. Just because I thought it was right for me, I can't ask someone to…leave what they've known most, if not all, of their lives."

Ja, you can. Ask me. What if…what if I'm ready this time? Elizabeth opened her mouth to say the words. They were there. Just out of reach. But something held her back.

If she actually said them, and Moses said no… What if he rejected her? What if he…pitied her? Was it worth the risk?

"I've heard the Dew Drop—" Moses's eyes were somber, though his mouth hooked toward a smile "—the remote one, will be open again tomorrow. I don't know how you organized it so quickly and effectively. But I'm not surprised. You're an amazing woman, Beth." His gaze held hers for a moment, the young man who'd initially charmed her and the older one she'd fallen back in love with in its depth. But what was mainly there was regret. He turned back toward the dishwashing station. "I've got more work to do here before I leave, so I'd better get back to it."

Elizabeth was too numb to move. Failing in her attempt to swallow past the ache in the back of her throat, her words were a raspy whisper. "You need some help. I'll stay."

Moses shook his head. "*Nee.* It's late. I'm sure you started long before daylight. Just for a little longer, I'm still your employer, Beth. Go home." He turned on the water and began to work.

Elizabeth waited for the eruption of anger at being told what to do. For the retort to burst forth at Moses for exerting his control over her. It wasn't there. What was was emptiness.

Concerned her legs wouldn't hold her, Elizabeth kept a hand on the counter as she moved along it. Turning toward the alley door, she spied the items she'd carried in what seemed hours ago. Thankfully, none of them required attention tonight. Even if they did, for the first time she could remember, Elizabeth didn't care about the restaurant.

The chains of the porch swing creaked as Elizabeth settled onto its white painted boards. Onyx rose to her feet, tail wagging hopefully. Elizabeth regarded her briefly before extending an open palm at the edge of the barely swaying swing. The dog strolled over to set her chin on it. Elizabeth gently scratched her underneath it. With a sigh, Onyx lowered her hindquarters to lean against the swing, stopping its motion.

"You're grayer than I am. Does it bring wisdom?" With her free hand, Elizabeth touched a strand of her hair where it disappeared into her *kapp*. "It hasn't seemed to have done that for me. If it had, maybe I'd know what to do.

"He has reason, you know. Reason not to trust me. Or he had. *Ja.* He was right. For sure and certain, I was upset he'd bought the restaurant. There *were* times I wanted him to leave. But I didn't sabotage him. And now that he's leaving? I'd do about anything to get him to stay."

She rubbed a thumb over the dog's silky head as lightning flickered in the distant darkness, soundlessly lighting up the horizon. At least, with no sound she could hear. Maybe the dog could.

"Looks like it's going to storm. Seems fitting. I'm finally getting what I want, total control over the restaurant—well, except for appeasing Bishop Weaver. And it...it doesn't feel like I thought it would. It doesn't bring the satisfaction, the comfort, the pleasure I'd expected." The distant flashes continued. A few moments later, the faint echo of thunder reached her.

"He did, though. Bring satisfaction. In arguing with him, in working with him. In just being with him." Elizabeth stared out at her snug little farm, its landscape intermittently illuminated by the lightning. "He keeps telling me to go home. This has been home for the past four-plus decades." She smiled wryly. "Though for several months, I've spent about as much time at the Dew Drop as here. And while that's been *gut*, it was even better when Moses was there. It won't be the same when he leaves. It will feel... empty. Many things will feel empty. Is this all there is for me now?"

There was no question of thunder accompanying the flashes of light. Elizabeth found herself counting the seconds between the lightning and the sound of thunder and dividing by five to estimate how many miles away the storm was.

"I wanted him to ask me to marry him again. I was going to say yes this time. Say yes to trusting him. If he'd asked again, it would prove he loved me, wouldn't it?" Onyx nudged Elizabeth's hand when her fingers paused their petting. "Or am I just giving him another test? He sold me the restaurant when he knew I wanted it. For sure and certain, it was at a loss for him. That's not a *gut* business decision. If not for business, why did he do it? And he cleared the way with the bishop for me to have it." Her lips twisted. "Now that I do, I want him instead. Maybe this is a test for me. Why should I force him to make such a critical decision for both of us?"

A few raindrops splattered on Elizabeth's cheek. Her skin prickled at the abrupt cool, damp breeze that swept over the porch.

Or perhaps it had prickled at the idea that struck her, much like the approaching lightning that stabbed into the horizon.

"Can I have both?" Elizabeth hissed in a breath at a particularly close flash. To execute this plan, she'd make herself vulnerable. She curled her fingers more deeply into Onyx's deep fur. But could being vulnerable to Moses and the pain and fear of rejection be any worse than the heartache she knew she'd have when he left her again?

She rose from the swing. Onyx stayed sitting, eyeing

her with resignation. Elizabeth frowned at the Labrador as lightning flashes continued to light up the night. Some dogs didn't like storms. Would Onyx be afraid out here? Wisconsin experienced significant spring storms and this was looking like it could be one of them. Did she have enough shelter here on the porch? Did she know enough to go to the shed to get out of the coming weather?

Elizabeth crossed her arms over her chest. Maybe she should walk Onyx over there and shut her in for the night. Fat droplets of rain splashed onto the porch steps. Lightning and the responding thunder were almost simultaneous. She'd be drenched by the time she got back to the house, if she wasn't struck by a bolt in the process.

With a sigh, Elizabeth opened the door to the kitchen. "Come on." Though she briefly hesitated, Onyx, wearing a doggy smile, needed no further urging. Elizabeth followed the dog inside and shut the door. She shook her head. "I'll be bringing Scarlett in from the barn next."

Moses sighed as he left the bank. It was done. A dream decades in the making was destroyed in a matter of days. Almost faster than the prompt repairs to the Dew Drop could be completed. Though all but painting was done, he'd determined to close the restaurant today to finish the work.

When the restaurant opened tomorrow, with its temporary hood-free menu, it would be without him.

He fingered the check he'd just collected before securing it. While he'd stayed at the restaurant yesterday with the repairs, Beth had been at the concession stand all day. He hadn't seen her since she'd agreed to buy the restaurant. Their only communication was her note left in his office informing him payment and paperwork were ready at the bank.

Would someone who truly loved a man put him through a test to prove that love? Moses figured he'd proved it by coming back. With the work Beth had arranged and done over the past few days, for a moment the other night, he'd thought—his lips twisted, he'd *wanted* to think—it meant something for him. Then he'd reminded himself she'd do almost anything for the restaurant. It was always the restaurant.

He'd arrived full of hopes. He was leaving empty, except for his bank account now. But even that was less than when he'd started. He wasn't used to failure. His expectations, his father's, pressed that trying wasn't enough. He'd had to succeed. What was his worth if he didn't meet those expectations?

Maybe that was why he'd fallen for Beth so long ago. She hadn't had any expectation of him. She didn't even *want* to be taken care of. With her, he hadn't had to be anyone but who he was. Or so he'd thought. Apparently, who he was wasn't someone she'd felt she could fully trust—then or now.

Wasn't there some saying about it being better to have tried and failed than never having tried at all? Or was that loved? Better to have loved and lost than never to have loved at all? Moses's shoulders sagged. He'd done both. Tried and failed, and loved and lost. Twice on that one. And if this was how "better" was supposed to feel, he wasn't sure he wanted any of it. But he didn't blame Beth. It was all his doing. She'd never asked him to return.

At a called greeting, Moses automatically lifted a hand to wave before he paused to turn and watch the passing buggy. Why were Samuel and his wife driving out of town in one conveyance when he'd arranged for the horse trader to pick up the rented horse and borrowed buggy?

With a frown, Moses hastened to the alley behind the restaurant. His steps slowed when he saw Daniel taking a filled hay net in to the gelding that should've been heading out of town along with the Schrocks. He followed him inside the shed.

"Where's Samuel going? Why's he leaving without the horse and buggy? He was to take them home today."

"Well, they are home. At least, the gelding is, temporarily. I bought him." Daniel ran a hand down the horse's sleek neck. "And Samuel is loaning me the buggy until I get my own."

"What are you talking about? You don't need a horse and buggy here. We've got bus tickets to take us back to Ohio."

"Hope you can get a refund for mine. I'm staying." Though his tone was mild, Daniel's jaw was firm.

Moses stared at his son, noticing for the first time that Daniel no longer had the slimness of a youth, but the breadth of a man. When had that happened? He folded his arms over his chest. "To do what? There's nothing for you here. I've sold the restaurant."

"Rebecca is here."

Moses closed his eyes as his stomach clenched. He'd encouraged the relationship between Daniel and Rebecca. Had even been thrilled as it had unfolded, seeing it as an echo of his and Elizabeth's early relationship.

Daniel wanted to stay for Rebecca. Would *he* have stayed if Elizabeth had said it was a condition of marrying him? But she'd never even given him that chance. "Rebecca is a *wunderbar* girl. I can see why you like her. But there are girls in Ohio."

"How can you say that? You know it's not the same. You'd hinted you and Beth had a past. You loved her, didn't you? That's why you came back."

Moses winced. "Sometimes love isn't enough. Not if it's one-sided. If Rebecca loves you, marry her here and have her come with us to Ohio."

"She wants to stay with her family. She has a sibling less than a year old she wants to see grow up. I want to stay because I love her and it's what she wants. You don't need me in Ohio. Between you, my sisters, my aunts and their husbands, you won't even miss me."

"What are you going to do up here for a living?"

Daniel smiled. "I'm going to manage the Dew Drop with Rebecca."

Scowling, Moses shook his head. "Beth will never give up management of the restaurant."

Daniel's smile expanded. "That's interesting to hear, considering she just hired us. With part of our payment being lodging. After we're married, of course."

"What lodging? The building has a second floor, but it's not set up for an apartment. And I doubt Beth has finances to remodel it. Not anymore, at least."

"We'll be living in her house in the country."

"Her house! Where's she going to live? Why isn't she managing *her* restaurant? What is she doing?" Moses leaned back against the shed's wooden wall. Maybe even with the Dew Drop sold, the stress *was* getting to him. He was totally confused. Contrary woman! He'd just sold Beth the restaurant, giving her what she'd always wanted.

Daniel's shoulders lifted in an innocent shrug. "Maybe you should ask her."

Moses's gaze narrowed at the glint in his son's eye. "Maybe I will." For the first time since entering the shed, he noticed the mare quietly munching hay on the other side of the gelding. "Where is she?"

"Where do you think?" Daniel tipped his head toward the restaurant.

Moses straightened abruptly and slipped past the gelding to the rear of the shed. Before stepping into the alley, he turned and looked back. "You're wrong, you know."

Daniel cocked his head.

"I will miss you, son. Immensely."

Moses hissed in a breath as he crossed the narrow alley. Daniel was staying in Wisconsin? Elizabeth had hired him to manage the restaurant and live in her house? What was the woman up to? He'd given her about everything he could think of. His pride, the restaurant…his heart. He gritted his teeth. Did she have to take his son as well?

He jerked the back door open and strode into the repaired kitchen. A quick visual sweep found it empty. At a telltale creak, Moses stopped in the doorway of the office to scowl at the back of Beth's *kapp* as she sat in the old chair, the pencil in her hand moving swiftly over paperwork on the desk.

Though she had to have heard him, she didn't turn around. Stubborn woman. "What are you doing?"

"Employee schedule. It's a necessary part of the business. Surely you understand that." She spoke to the papers in front of her.

"You know what I mean. What are you doing hiring Daniel and Rebecca to run the restaurant that you just bought? And telling them they can live in your house?"

Beth sat up until the back facing him was as straight as a pitchfork handle. "Because they can. Once I make them, I keep my promises." She tapped the pencil in her hand against the paperwork on the desk. Her shoulders lifted in a deep inhalation. "I have a…proposal for you."

Moses frowned. "The price of the restaurant isn't changing, either up or down. I've already got the check." Though the price now seemed too high, with the additional cost of his son. The continual drum of the pencil drew Moses's attention. His gaze sharpened on the end of it, where teeth marks marred the upper length. Beth had been chewing on the pencil. She was nervous. His brows furrowed. She should be feeling triumphant. Celebratory. Jubilant. She'd gotten what she wanted. So why was she nervous?

The obvious sign of her agitation eased some of his own. An agitated Beth was a very interesting one. Moses leaned a shoulder against the doorjamb. "But I'm listening."

Tap, tap, tap. "I was wondering about a…business arrangement."

His lips twitched. Was that really Beth in the chair? Beth didn't "wonder"—she demanded, she told, she instructed. "I don't talk business to the back of someone's head."

The old chair squeaked as she twisted around to face him. It was indeed Beth, but one with wary eyes in a pale face. Beth had definite thoughts on business, in which she was seldom wary or pale. Could this business arrangement include a more personal one? Though his posture against the door frame remained nonchalant, tension thrummed through Moses.

"I'm planning to…um…be an absentee owner. I've learned it can be done if the in-house management is *gut*." She frowned. "Well, somewhat *gut*."

Moses's heart was racing. "Where do you plan to go?"

"That depends." He'd seen a variety of expressions in Beth's brown eyes before: energy, intelligence, ferocity, determination. But seldom vulnerability. Her lips parted; her chest rose and fell on a series of rapid breaths.

His own breath was getting short. But this time Moses

didn't panic. For it wasn't pain, fear or dread that filled him. It was hope. "On?"

"On whether someone will ask me to go with him." Her throat bobbed in a swallow. "Again."

In the normal cacophony of a busy kitchen, he wouldn't have heard the whisper. Moses was glad the room behind him was as silent as a tomb so he could absorb the words he'd waited over two decades to hear.

At his continued silence, her gaze tightened from wary to a growing fierceness. "So, will you do it?"

He shrugged a shoulder. "I don't know. You'd be a scary business partner. You set fire to my restaurant."

"It's *my* restaurant." She was no longer whispering.

Moses struggled to keep a grin from his face. "It wasn't at the time."

Beth studied him intently before sighing. "Are you ever going to forgive me?"

He tilted his head in consideration. "For this one, maybe. Not for the other."

"What other?"

Moses reached down to grab her fisted hands and pull her to her feet. "For setting fire to my heart years ago and never putting it out." He wrapped his arms around her unresisting form and pulled her close. It felt like coming home. "Beth, my Beth. Will you marry me? Go with me to Ohio? Be my partner in business and in life?"

There was no question now of what was in her eyes. It was pure joy. Along with a few tears. "Yes, yes and yes. I was afraid you'd never ask again."

"I was just waiting for the right time." He kissed her. Something else he'd been waiting for, for a long time.

She sighed and rested her head on his shoulder. "We're going to argue."

"Absolutely. I'm looking forward to it." Moses felt her smile against his neck. "You know," he murmured into her ear, "I never liked scrapple. I just ate it because you liked to make it for me."

Beth's arms remained entwined about him as she leaned back to meet his gaze. "That's *gut*, because if you want it now, you'll have to make it yourself. I won't make it for you."

"You know what you will make me, Beth?"

Elizabeth eyed him warily. "What?"

"Happy. You make me happy."

Epilogue

Elizabeth swallowed as, through the tinted windows of the van, she spotted the large gathering on the porch. Her hand tightened around Moses's.

"What if they don't like me?"

He gave her fingers a reassuring squeeze. "When has that ever stopped you?"

"Well, this is your family."

"I know. And I know they'll grow to love you as much as I do. *Ach*, almost as much. You gained Daniel's affection, didn't you? And he'd be the toughest nut to crack."

"It helped that I gave him a job."

"You know he liked you before then."

"I suppose so. Do you think they'll be upset that Daniel saw us wed and they didn't?"

"*Nee.* There're a lot of women in my family. They'll think I did the right thing by marrying you in your home district so all your friends and family could come."

Beth smiled. "It was quite a crowd, wasn't it?"

"*Ja.* And for once, you didn't have to cook for it."

"I guess that makes it my favorite wedding, then."

Moses lifted their clasped hands to kiss the back of hers. "Is that the only reason?"

She drew a gentle finger along his cheek. "Well, it was certainly one worth waiting for."

"See, no arguing yet. We continue to be in agreement on things. Are you ready?"

Beth inhaled deeply. "I guess I'll have to be. It's a bit of a drive back to Wisconsin and the house would be rather crowded now with Daniel and Rebecca married and living there as well."

"Let's go, then." He slid from his seat to slide open the door. The hired driver stayed inside as Moses and Beth exited the rented van. When Onyx, after a brief hesitation, jumped down beside them, Beth wasted no time in stroking the dog's silky head for reassurance.

The gathering on the porch flowed down the steps and enveloped them. Beth found herself meeting Moses's sisters, brothers-in-law, his children and the spouses of the ones who were married. The introductions became a blur. She didn't remember any names except for Jonathan, his ten-year-old son. No one seemed to mind. Everyone was hugging, smiling and chattering.

Her breath caught when someone handed her a *boppeli*. Her arms automatically curled around the warm weight of the infant. Moses smiled down at the sleeping baby.

"That's one of my grandchildren. I've got a few now." His gaze was warm as he looked over the boisterous crowd. "You've just become a wife. Can you handle immediately being a *mamm* and *grossmammi* to so many as well?"

"Ja." Her heart full, Elizabeth smiled at her new husband. "I'm a capable woman, remember."

Moses wrapped an arm around her shoulders. "That you are."

"How about you? You went north to expand your business. Though not as you imagined, you have added a restaurant to the fold after all. Isn't that success?"

Elizabeth blushed as Moses tipped his head to kiss her in full view of his family. "I've added a wife and my love to my life. I call that the greatest success I could ever hope for."

* * * * *

Dear Reader,

Thank you so much for making the journey to Miller's Creek with me, this time to the Dew Drop!

I knew nothing about the restaurant business, except that I like to eat in one occasionally. So many folks have been so helpful in sharing their knowledge. When the waiter asked our table if we needed anything else, I'm sure he didn't expect questions about the restaurant's kitchen. I certainly didn't expect the manager to come out and spend twenty minutes answering my questions and giving me a quick tour of the kitchen. Also the gentleman at the St. Francois County Health Department, who spent some time discussing potential troubles for my fictional restaurant kitchen when I unexpectedly showed up at the department window. Both were reminders that people can be so kind and helpful. They're inspirations for me to be the same.

To keep updated on the next trip to Miller's Creek, stop by jocelynmcclay.com (where you can sign up for my newsletter) or visit me on Facebook.

May God bless you,
Jocelyn McClay